Alex

TWILIGHT FALLS BOOK ONE

A.M. SALINGER

COPYRIGHT

NIGHTS

One Night - 1

The Escort - 2

Tokyo Heat - 3

Sweet Obsession - 4

Sweet Possession - 5

The Proposition - 6

Undisclosed - 7

Hush - 8

One Day - 9

TWILIGHT FALLS

Alex - 1

Carter - 2

Hunter - 3

Wyatt - 4

Drake - 5

Tristan - 6

Miles - 7

ALEX HANCOCK CAME OUT OF THE COFFEE SHOP opposite the courthouse and froze in his tracks.

Someone had parked their dirty, mud-streaked Jeep Wrangler close to his pristine, black and red Triumph motorcycle.

Alex's knuckles whitened on his cup of black coffee. *When it rains, it fucking pours!*

He stormed across the street, stopped in front of the offending vehicle, and glared at it as if it had committed a crime. A car slowly pulled up behind him.

"Wow," someone murmured. "You look pissed."

Alex turned. A pretty brunette was watching him with an amused expression from behind the wheel of a red, convertible Mini.

"You would be too if some asshole just blocked you in!" he snapped.

Izzy Batista's green eyes sparkled impishly as she observed the grimy, four-wheel drive. "Yup, that guy must be one giant dick."

She parked her car and joined him outside the courthouse.

"I gotta give it to you, Hancock. You sure scrub up nice." Izzy placed her hands on her hips and scrutinized him with a critical eye.

Alex sighed irritably and downed his drink. He winced when a burst of acid rose in his throat.

"Easy on the coffee, stud," Izzy murmured. "We don't want you getting an ulcer on your big day."

A fresh bout of nerves twisted Alex's gut at Izzy's words.

"I can't believe I'm doing this," he mumbled to himself. "Me, Alex Hancock, getting married."

Izzy patted his arm. "No backsies." A trace of steel underscored her friendly tone. "Remember, you got a lot riding on this."

He crushed the coffee cup and tossed it in a nearby trash can.

She's right.

It had been a month since the life Alex had carefully built in San Diego had come crashing down around him, after his business partner of two years embezzled from their law firm and ran off to Mexico. Mired in debt and with his new condo on the verge of being repossessed, Alex had desperately been trying to raise the necessary capital to salvage his career and company when Izzy Batista had called him out of the blue ten days ago. The sister of Wyatt Batista, one of Alex's lifelong friends from his hometown of Twilight Falls, Izzy had discovered the predicament he was in through her older brother.

"I may have a solution to your problems," Izzy said. "Word of warning though, it's pretty unorthodox."

Alex stilled where he sat on his couch, his cell phone in hand. "What do you mean?"

"One of my clients is in trouble," Izzy said. "They have to get married by the end of the month or they'll lose their estate and half of their considerable fortune."

Alex frowned. "I don't understand."

Izzy sighed. "I'm saying this client needs a mail-order groom. And pronto. They're willing to pay half a million dollars to the right candidate."

Alex's mouth went dry. "Half a million dollars?" His heart pounded against his ribs as he glanced at the boxes filling the apartment. He'd barely started unpacking when Ryan had pulled the rug out from under him and disappeared with half the company's funds.

"Yup, half a million dollars," Izzy repeated. "The contract's for six months. Marry the client, live with them, and then walk into the sunset with the money and no strings attached."

Alex swallowed, shocked that he was even entertaining the crazy idea Izzy had just proposed.

"Where does your client live?" he mumbled.

"Twilight Falls."

Alex grimaced at Izzy's answer. He raked a hand through his hair and stared at the dazzling lights of San Diego Bay through the glass doors overlooking his terrace, a storm of memories and bittersweet emotions crashing over him.

"I know you don't like coming back here, Alex," Izzy said quietly. "Not since the accident. But this could solve all your problems. And my client's too."

Alex chewed the inside of his cheek. "What's wrong with your client?"

"What makes you think there's anything wrong with my client?" Izzy said in a voice that Alex immediately distrusted.

"Because someone with that much money shouldn't be struggling to find herself a fiancé, even a fake one. So what is it? Is she unattractive? Does she have a horrible personality?" He pulled a face. "Does she eat puppies for breakfast?"

"None of the above," Izzy replied in a cheerful tone. "The client is gorgeous. They're just a bit...eccentric, is all."

Alex mulled Izzy's words over. Eccentric he could deal with.

"Are they expecting sex?"

A soft chuckle travelled down the line.

"No, it isn't that kind of arrangement. Besides, I know you're more into dicks than vaginas."

"Yeah, well, my dick hasn't seen much action lately," Alex muttered.

"And here I thought you moved to San Diego for all the gay guys," Izzy said drily. "You know, since you'd pretty much fucked all the hot ones here in Twilight Falls."

Alex scowled. "I only fucked one hot guy in that town."

Izzy laughed. Alex found his lips curving in a faint smile at her bubbly voice. Truth be told, he missed Izzy and Wyatt. He missed all the friends he'd left behind when he decided to move to San Diego, after the accident that had changed all of their lives.

A comfortable silence settled between them.

"So, what will it be, Alex?" Izzy finally said.

Alex hesitated. "The end of the month is only ten days away."

"Your math is spot on. I knew there was a reason why you became a lawyer."

Alex ignored her sarcastic words. "Give me a few days to think about it."

It had taken him three days to make his decision. Six days later, he'd put his stuff in storage, returned his apartment keys to his realtor, and climbed on the beautifully restored, classic motorcycle he'd owned since he was seventeen for the one-hundred-and-fifty-mile ride to the San Bernardino Mountains and the quaint, historic town of Twilight Falls.

Nestled in a valley of towering pine forests and home to the picturesque waterfall and rapids from which it took its name, Twilight Falls started life as a nineteenth-century trading post and mining settlement, during the California Gold Rush. After a slump following the two World Wars, the place saw a strong revival in the second half of the twentieth century, as a result of a sustained campaign by the city council to turn it into a tourist town. The rise in outdoor sports activities meant it now stayed busy pretty much all year around, with the briefest of lulls at Thanksgiving and the New Year.

Alex had reached Twilight Falls late last night. Having refused Izzy and Wyatt's offer to put him up at their place, he'd booked himself into a motel outside town; the spring tourist season was just getting started and there'd still been rooms available at short notice. Not that he would have wanted to stay in town. Even though it had been twelve years since he'd left the place, he was bound to bump into someone he knew and he wasn't in the mood for small talk.

"Are you ready?" Izzie said presently, excitement raising the pitch of her voice.

"Not really," Alex murmured.

Izzy grinned. "Yeah, well, if you'd stayed at our place, we could have gotten you wasted and you'd be doing this drunk right now."

"I really don't think the county clerk would be impressed if the groom turned up with a hangover," Alex said sternly. "Besides, I'm entering a legal agreement with this woman. The least I can do is show up sober."

He looked up at the two-story, cream stucco and red-brick building before them and squared his shoulders.

Whoever this broad is, I only have to live with her for six months. How bad can it be?

An odd expression danced across Izzy's face.

"What is it?" Alex said.

"Nothing." Izzy flashed him a bright smile, hooked her arm through his elbow, and guided him up the short flight of steps and into the building.

They checked in at reception and headed in the direction of the court rooms. Surprise darted through Alex when Izzy walked past the austere wooden doors and continued down the hall.

"Where are we going?" he said, puzzled.

"To the chapel," Izzy replied breezily.

He arched an eyebrow.

"The client insisted," she explained with a mysterious smile.

The first tendrils of unease started coiling through Alex. Izzy was acting strange. And he wasn't sure he liked the hint of devilment in the depths of her eyes.

The chapel doors appeared up ahead. Alex's pulse speeded up when they opened them and stepped inside a large, airy chamber. The chapel was a relatively new addition to the courthouse and had been designed along the traditional lines of a church, with an altar, a chancel, and a nave split by a central aisle. But it wasn't the charming ecclesiastical interior or the delightful pastel colors around them that caused Alex to draw a sharp breath and rock to a stop on the checkered marble flooring.

He stared beyond the bright posies and white lace decorating the wooden pews to the two figures rising to their feet from the front right row.

"Jesus, Izzy!" Alex hissed, shock reverberating through him. "I can't marry her! She's older than my grandmother!"

The elderly dame in the pink brocade dress and pale floral hat arched an eyebrow.

"You were right," she told Izzy. "That one has a smart mouth on him." The woman's eyes fairly twinkled with glee as she studied Alex's stunned expression. "I'm not the one you're marrying, sonny."

Alex's heart stuttered. His gaze switched to the tall, dark-haired man in the smart, navy-blue suit and the ivory, rose boutonnière next to the woman. A thunderous expression clouded the stranger's handsome, stubbled features.

Shit. You're kidding me.

"What the hell is going on, Izzy?" the man growled.

CHAPTER TWO

Finn West glared at his art consultant.

Izzy Batista blinked her green eyes innocently at him. "Why, you're getting married, Finn."

Finn observed the striking blond man next to Izzy. The guy was wearing a light azure three-piece suit with a crisp white shirt and a silver-gray silk tie. The outfit highlighted his pale blue eyes, which were currently wide and filled with the same angry bewilderment coursing through Finn.

"He's a man!" Finn snarled.

The stranger next to Izzy stiffened as if he'd been slapped.

Finn ignored the icy look dawning on the man's face, clenched his jaw, and directed an accusing stare at his great-aunt.

"Did you know about this?"

Margaret Fontanier-West, or Aunt Maggie as Finn called her, smiled beatifically.

"Yes, I did. The terms of my demands did not

include details of the sex of the person you had to marry."

"Besides," Izzy added, "I quite clearly recall you telling me that you didn't care if it was a man or a woman you got hitched to."

Finn swallowed a curse. He couldn't believe Izzy and his great-aunt had concocted this plot together.

And damnit, she's right. I did say that!

He winced internally as he recalled the drunken conversation he'd had with Izzy when he'd rang the art consultant for advice late one night, some eleven days ago.

"Your great-aunt has done what?!" Izzy gasped.

"She's given me an ultimatum," Finn mumbled, head throbbing and hand clasped around his third glass of bourbon. "She wants me to get married by the end of the month or she'll revoke the family trust. Which means I'll lose the house and half of my investments."

Silence fell on the other end of the line.

"Izzy, you there?" Finn said.

"Yeah, I'm here."

Relief filled Finn. In the three years since he'd lost his wife Catherine, Izzy was the first woman he'd come to consider as a friend. It was through the owner of an art gallery in L.A. that he'd gotten to know her. Much to Finn's amazement, Izzy had grown up in Twilight Falls, the place he and Catherine had moved to five years ago, before she fell ill.

After a stint in Paris and New York, Izzy had returned to California and her home roots. Finn had hired her to work for him in her capacity as an art consultant eight months ago. In that time, he'd come to appreciate her vivacious personality and her brains.

"What will you do?" Izzy said.

Despair twisted through Finn, his mind still spinning from the bombshell the woman who had raised him had dropped that afternoon.

"I don't know," he said bitterly. "I've already spoken to my lawyers. Aunt Maggie is within her rights to dissolve the trust."

"Even though you've been pouring money into it through your stock investments?" Izzy said sharply. "I mean, most of that wealth is yours, isn't it?"

"Yeah," Finn murmured. "Catherine and I chose to make her our trustee five years ago. Neither of us had any other family and—" he paused, emotion clogging his throat for a moment, "and we couldn't have children."

"I know you won't like hearing this, but I kinda understand why your great-aunt is doing this," Izzy murmured after a while. "You do too, don't you?"

Finn stiffened.

"Even though I've been out of town for a while, even I've heard the gossip, Finn," Izzy continued. "You've hardly set foot outside your estate since Catherine's death. And you've barely spoken to anyone bar me, your aunt, and your housekeeper in the time since I've known you. If it wasn't for your art, the world would forget Finn West ever existed."

"Maybe that's a good thing," Finn murmured.

A frustrated sigh echoed down the line.

"I don't know what happened between you and your wife, but nothing you could have done justifies what you've put yourself through since her death, Finn," Izzy said in a hard

voice. "It's about damn time you actually started living again."

Finn swallowed, the age-old regret and bitterness that had been a chain around his heart for the last ten years swirling inside him.

"That's the thing, Izzy."

"What?" she said, puzzled.

"I didn't do anything."

Izzy blew out a sigh. "Boy, you're really wasted, aren't you?"

Finn knocked his bourbon back and grimaced as the alcohol burned a fiery path down his throat. Anguish turned to anger when he recalled his great-aunt's cool words once more.

"All right!" he growled. "She wants me to get married? I'll get married! I don't care if it's a man or a woman, I just need a name on a damn marriage license by the end of this month! And I'm willing to pay good money for it too. Half a million dollars should do it."

Izzy gasped. "You're kidding, right?! Jesus, Finn, just how much have you had to drink?"

"I'm not joking," Finn said in a hard voice. "Will you help me, Izzy?"

"Are you serious?!"

"Yes." Finn grimaced and rubbed the back of his neck. "Look, I have zero interest in checking out the dating scene and trying to find myself a fake fiancée. Once I do this, Aunt Maggie will hopefully leave me the hell alone."

"Wow. It's a good thing you're not going on the dating scene. That stellar attitude of yours won't win you any favors." Izzy paused. "Okay, I'll see what I can do. In fact—"

her tone turned thoughtful, "I just heard of someone who might be in need of some urgent cash."

Finn dragged a hand down his face. Izzy had kept her promise. He couldn't deny that. He just hadn't expected her to take his words literally. When she'd called him a week ago and told him she'd arranged a marriage license and to turn up at the courthouse today for his wedding with a contract for his new spouse, Finn had presumed the latter would be a woman. He studied the vexed blond next to the art consultant and wondered where she'd magicked the poor schmuck from. The guy looked about ready to spit nails.

And probably hammer them straight through my and Izzy's corpses.

The county clerk who was to officiate Finn's marriage strolled into the room.

"Are we ready?" the woman asked with a cheerful grin.

"Not quite," Finn muttered.

"Heck no!" Blond Guy stated vehemently.

The clerk's expression fell.

"Oh." She pursed her lips. "Having last minute doubts?" She glanced from Finn to the blond. "If it's any consolation, you two make a cute couple."

Izzy muffled a snort behind one hand. Finn practically heard Blond Guy grit his teeth.

"Could I have a moment with my—" the man made a pained expression, *"fiancé* and our witnesses?"

"Sure thing," the clerk replied with a smile. "Take

your time. There's an hour left until the next civil ceremony."

Blond Guy stormed out of the chapel, an unrepentant-looking Izzy on his heels. Finn headed reluctantly after them with his great-aunt.

"I like him," Aunt Maggie stated. "He's plucky. I bet he's a firecracker in the bedroom."

A strangled groan left Finn. "I can't believe you just said that!"

Aunt Maggie gave him a stern look. "I may be old, but my eyes still work. If I were thirty years younger, I'd take him for a spin myself. I mean, have you seen his buns? They're mighty—"

Finn put his hand up. "Please, just—just stop talking!" he begged.

Aunt Maggie chuckled. "You're so straight-laced. I don't know where you get it from. It certainly isn't from my side of the family." She patted Finn on the back, her eyes gleaming with a light that caused a shiver to run down his spine. "You need to learn to relax, Finn. Enjoy life while you still can. Do the things you've never dared do before."

Finn couldn't help but feel there was some kind of hidden meaning behind her words. Blond Guy's voice reached his ears as they stepped into the hall.

The man was admonishing Izzy in a low voice brimming with fury.

"I can't believe this!" he hissed. "Why the hell did you tell me your client was a woman when he's quite clearly a man?!"

Izzy blinked innocently. "I never said my client was a woman."

Blond Guy's mouth fell open. "What?!" he spluttered.

Finn's gaze dropped to the man's perfectly shaped Cupid bow and sculptured lips.

"I never said my client was a woman," Izzy repeated patiently. "You just assumed that *he*—" she looked over at Finn, "was a she."

A glazed expression washed across Blond Guy's face. "Shit!" He glanced at Finn. "Well, *he* quite clearly didn't know he was gonna get hitched to a dude either!"

Finn narrowed his eyes. "*He* has a name. And *he* is standing right here."

Blond Guy blew out a sigh. "Look, Mr.—?" He arched an eyebrow at Finn.

"Mr. West," Finn replied coolly. "Finn West."

"Look, Mr. West," Blond Guy said briskly, "surely, you don't want to go ahead with this? I mean, it's clear you were expecting to marry a woman today!"

"I was," Finn admitted.

Relief darkened Blond Guy's eyes. "Great!" He turned to Izzy. "I really don't know what you were thinking but I'm calling this—"

"I still want to marry you."

Blond Guy froze. He turned stiffly and looked at Finn as if he'd grown horns and a forked tail.

Finn stared back, not sure who was the most shocked out of the two of them at the words he'd just blurted out. He registered Izzy's surprised expression and Aunt Maggie's thoughtful stare. He ignored the two women and kept his gaze locked on the stunned blue eyes opposite him.

"You're obviously in some kind of financial trouble, otherwise you wouldn't have agreed to this. And I need a spouse." Finn cast a dark glance at his great-aunt before looking at Blond Guy once more. "Let's make the best of this situation. After all, it's only for six months."

A muscle jumped in Blond Guy's jawline. He observed Finn with a frown, his expression clearly conflicted.

A wicked impulse Finn never even knew he possessed suddenly took hold of him. He pasted a cocky half-smile on his face, stuck his hands in his pants pockets, and closed the distance to Blond Guy at a leisurely pace. The man's citrusy cologne hit Finn's nostrils when he stopped in front of him. Blond Guy tilted his chin and glared at Finn. Finn's lips twitched. He had a good two inches on the man. By the looks of it, Blond Guy wasn't too happy about that.

"So, what's your answer?"

CHAPTER THREE

I have lost my fucking mind. There's no other way to explain this.

Alex scowled as he followed Finn's Jeep up the winding mountain road. As Fate would have it, the man he'd just married during what had to be the strangest day of his life was the owner of the vehicle that had blocked his bike in at the courthouse.

And now, here I am, being led to God knows where by a potential mad man!

He still couldn't believe he'd fallen for Finn's unspoken challenge a few hours ago. When Izzy's client had walked up to him with an arrogant air and practically dared him to go ahead with their farce of a wedding, Alex had wanted nothing more than to turn around and hightail it the hell out of that courthouse and Twilight Falls.

But something in Finn West's eyes had piqued Alex's interest. He still wasn't sure what it was, or what had made him stand his ground and accept the man's offer.

There was one thing Alex couldn't deny. And it only added to his growing irritation at the situation he now found himself in.

Izzy was right. The guy's gorgeous.

Finn's taillights flashed as he slowed. He flipped his indicator and steered the Jeep onto a private road that disappeared into the forest. Alex headed after him, intrigued; he'd not explored this part of the forest around Twilight Falls before.

A wrought-iron security gate appeared at the end of the muddy, wooded lane. Finn entered a code in the panel on the post on the side of the path and drove the Jeep through the gateway.

Alex revved the Triumph's engine and kept up. Cream gravel crunched under their tires as they negotiated a canopy-covered approach. The trees gradually cleared ahead. They crested a rise.

Alex drew a sharp breath and braked to a stop.

The land dipped before him to form a shallow valley overlooking a gully with a gurgling brook and a creek. Looming out of the forest at the bottom of the gentle incline was a beautiful, modern, wood and glass house. Set over two stories and topped by gray slate tiles, it blended beautifully into its stunning surroundings.

That doesn't look like a bad place to be stuck in for six months.

Alex rode down the slope after Finn and pulled into

a graveled forecourt. He parked his motorcycle next to Finn's Jeep just as the man got out of the vehicle. Alex climbed off the Triumph, removed his helmet, and raked a hand through his tousled hair.

"When was this place built?" he said curiously as he studied the building's contemporary frontage.

"Five years ago," Finn replied.

Anger surged through Alex at Finn's curt tone.

"Look, I know neither of us wanted this, but if anyone deserves to be pissed right now, it's me," he said coldly. "I'm the one who just moved halfway across the state and got tricked into marrying you."

A muscle jumped in Finn's cheek.

Gravel crunched behind them, distracting them both.

Relief flooded Alex when he turned and saw Izzy's red Mini rolling down the driveway. Although he blamed Wyatt's kid sister for his current predicament, he was grateful she had decided to come to the estate with them. The tension between him and Finn was only growing with each passing hour and it didn't look like things were going to get better any time soon.

Izzy parked her car and popped her trunk open. Alex helped her unload the backpack he'd brought from San Diego and the suitcase he'd purchased in town. Now that he knew where he was going to be living for the next six months, he would arrange for some of his stuff to be delivered to the house. In the meantime, he'd bought enough clothes to last him the week.

Izzy pursed her lips in a faint pout as she looked from Alex to Finn. "I can't believe both of you refused to go for a celebratory lunch. Why don't I make you guys an early dinner?"

"This is a business arrangement, Izzy," Finn said coolly, letting himself inside the house. "There's nothing to celebrate."

"He's right." Alex frowned at Finn's disappearing back. "The last thing I feel like doing right now is celebrating."

Izzy took a bottle of champagne and a bag of groceries from the Mini's rear seat. "Well, if you guys aren't going to paint the town red, then I will!" She stormed past Alex, her expression determined.

Alex sighed. "You know you're driving, right?"

"I'm allowed one glass to commemorate your wedding," Izzy retorted. "Honestly, I don't know who's the bigger grouch of the two of you!"

Alex bit back a frustrated groan and followed her, his luggage in hand.

The interior of the house was nicer than he'd imagined, which ticked him off even more. A wide, airy vestibule topped with a glass roof branched out into an east and west corridor before leading to an open-plan living and dining room that spanned half the property's width and overlooked a deck out back. Thick pine forest filled the skyline beyond the sleek wood and steel terrace.

Alex dragged his gaze from the riveting landscape outside the floor-to-ceiling glass wall and put his stuff down. He followed the sounds of clanging pots and pans to a modern kitchen that opened out onto a sun-drenched veranda overlooking the creek.

Izzy had taken her pumps off and was muttering to herself while investigating the contents of several cabinets.

"Want a hand?" Alex said lightly.

He'd never been able to stay mad at Izzy for long and they both knew it.

"Nah." Izzy's face brightened when she finally spotted what she was looking for. "Aha!" She removed a pair of roasting pans from a drawer with a triumphant air. "Why don't you go check the place out?" Her eyes softened as she studied Alex's wary expression. "Knowing Finn, he's probably being a bear and hiding in his studio. Here, you might as well take this to him. God knows you two need something in you to lighten up the mood."

She popped open the champagne, filled two flutes, and handed them to him. Alex accepted the drinks gratefully before heading back into the lounge. His unease melted away as he started exploring the house that he was going to live in for the next six months.

From the limited conversation he'd had with Izzy after the wedding, Alex knew Finn was some kind of famous artist who'd moved to Twilight Falls when his wife was still alive. According to Izzy, the man had become a virtual recluse since his wife's death from ovarian cancer three years ago and now barely left his estate apart from the occasional short trip into town to get a haircut.

Well, whatever the guy's problem is, he definitely has good taste.

Finn had decorated the mansion with a sparse, eclectic collection of furniture and artwork. Though Alex recognized some of the exorbitant brands and paintings on display, his eyes were drawn to a select few sculptures scattered randomly around the place. The carvings, mostly of human figures, were made from various materials and evoked a feeling of deep sensuality.

Finn's studio was at the end of the west corridor.

Alex stilled when he opened the door and stepped inside what was effectively a giant glass box with a stone floor. He stared at the mesmerizing views of the forest and the brook beyond the walls before looking around.

There was no sign of Finn.

Alex hesitated before heading farther inside the room. He observed the tidy worktops and sink, an easel with a partial charcoal sketch of a woman's body, and a drape covering what looked to be Finn's current work in progress. He moved toward a shelf holding half a dozen trophies, feeling guilty at snooping around a perfect stranger's life.

A grimace twisted his lips at that thought. *Well, to be fair, he's my husband.*

Alex's eyes widened when he read the plaques on the trophies. They were all distinguished national and international art awards.

A picture stood at one end of the shelf. It showed Finn and a pretty, petite brunette with warm, hazel eyes standing next to the creek, the skeleton of what would become their house in the background behind them. The woman stood with her back to Finn and was grinning at the camera. Finn had his arms looped around her and his chin propped on top of her head, a contented smile on his face.

Alex studied the couple. It was clear to him from their body language that Finn and his wife had loved and respected each other. He frowned.

This is the only picture of them I've seen in the house so far though.

Alex exited the studio in a pensive mood and made his way back to the main living area. A glass and steel staircase rose past the open, circular fireplace. The steps curved up to a mezzanine and the second floor.

Alex wasn't surprised to discover that all the bedrooms and bathrooms were south facing to take advantage of the incredible views of the pine forest and the creek.

Whoever designed this place did a great job of making the most of its surroundings.

He navigated an airy passage dotted with more sculptures and paintings and spotted an empty room that he liked the look of. He opened the door of the bedroom next to it and froze on the threshold.

Finn stood barefoot in the middle of the carpeted floor, next to a king size bed. He had his back to Alex and was stripping out of his shirt, his imposing silhouette outlined against the dazzling greens of the trees and the blue sky beyond a glass wall.

Alex's mouth went dry.

Finn turned, his hands stilling on his belt buckle. A frown darkened his face.

Alex's pulse thumped in his veins as he met Finn's eyes.

"Here." He crossed the floor and handed the artist the second flute of champagne. "Izzy's orders."

Finn hesitated before blowing out a tired sigh. He took the glass, oblivious to the tension now coursing through Alex.

"Has Izzy always been this bossy?"

Alex told himself to focus on the question and not on Finn's six-pack or the strip of dark hair that arrowed alluringly down his abs before disappearing behind his belt buckle.

"Pretty much. She was worse when she was a kid." Alex swallowed. "I'm sorry, I'll leave you to get undressed." He twisted on his heels and made for the exit, suddenly eager to get the hell out of there. A thought came to him as he reached the threshold. He paused and looked over his shoulder at the man who stood silently watching him. "By the way, can I use the room next door?"

"Sure," Finn murmured with a shrug. "You can use any of the bedrooms."

"Thanks."

Alex left Finn's bedroom, walked down the corridor to the landing, and stopped at the top of the stairs. He drew a ragged breath, conscious of his arousal pressing uncomfortably against the zipper of his pants.

Shit. The strong, beautifully defined muscles of Finn's shoulders and back flashed in front of Alex's eyes. *How the hell does an artist get a body like that anyway?*

Alex hoped Finn hadn't noticed his body's reaction to his near-nakedness. Because one thing had just become abundantly clear. He was attracted to Finn West. And that could only mean a whole heap of trouble.

CHAPTER FOUR

"Excuse me?" Finn said blankly.

They had just finished dinner and were clearing the table. Izzy looked at them innocently from where she was stacking plates and cutlery in the dishwasher in Finn's kitchen.

Alex gazed open-mouthed at Izzy, his head spinning at the bombshell she'd just casually dropped.

"You two have to share the same bed," Izzy repeated. "It's a stipulation of the contract you signed this morning."

"What stipulation?!" Finn roared.

He stormed out of the kitchen and returned a moment later, a document in hand.

"Page two, section ten," Izzy said helpfully.

Finn rifled through the contract and went deathly still. He raised his head and narrowed accusing eyes at Izzy. "This wasn't here the last time I looked!"

Alex walked over to Finn and took the document off him. His stomach dropped as he studied the clause that had been added to the contract. It looked legal and above board.

"Finn's right." Alex frowned at Izzy. "Why the hell is this even in here?"

Izzy shrugged, looking for all the world as if she wasn't to be blamed for this latest mess.

"It was one of Aunt Maggie's last-minute requests. I'm kinda surprised you didn't notice, Alex." She smiled. "You're a lawyer after all."

Alex's frown turned into a full-blown scowl. "Yeah, well, in case you hadn't noticed, I've had other things on my mind lately!"

Finn stared at Alex. "You're a lawyer?"

"Yeah, I am," Alex replied testily. He scanned the rest of the document. "Christ. What's next? Is she gonna want a blood ceremony?" He glared at Izzy. "Is there another clause where someone turns up tomorrow and checks the bedsheets for evidence of my virginity?"

Finn swallowed the wrong way and choked on his breath.

"Oh, I think we both know the name of the guy who popped *your* cherry," Izzy declared tartly while Finn coughed.

Alex felt his cheeks grow warm.

Finn stopped coughing and stared at Alex, surprise widening his pupils. "You're gay?"

Alex stiffened. Though he knew Izzy would never have gotten him involved in this had she known Finn hated gays, he still tilted his chin challengingly at the other man.

"Yes, I am. You got a problem with that?"

Finn blinked, nonplussed. "No, I don't."

Alex turned to Izzy, not quite sure what it was he'd just read in Finn's dark gaze.

"And how exactly does Aunt Maggie intend to enforce this condition?" His tone turned acerbic. "Is she gonna install cameras? I mean, I'm all for a bit of kink in the bedroom, but this is taking things too far, don't you think?"

Izzy grinned. "Aunt Maggie and I know that you two are honorable men. She's counting on the fact that you'll keep your word."

"So, she's just going to trust that we'll actually sleep with each other?" Alex snapped.

He regretted his words instantly as a hot image flashed before his eyes. Of him in Finn's bed. Of him *under* Finn.

Yeah, like that would ever happen.

Izzy eyed Alex shrewdly, the smile playing on her lips telling him she'd guessed the filthy thought he'd just had. Alex swallowed a groan.

She is the devil.

"Sleep, not sleep." Izzy shrugged. "What happens between a husband and husband is their business."

Alex stifled a curse at the overt innuendo.

"Right, I'll be off, then." Izzy picked up her bag and headed for the exit. "Have a nice night, you two!"

Alex and Finn stared after her in the silence that followed.

Finn spat in the sink, rinsed his mouth, and patted his chin dry with a towel. He frowned at his reflection in the mirror before turning and heading in the bedroom, still maddened at this latest plot twist in his great-aunt's machinations.

What the hell is Aunt Maggie thinking? What is sharing a bed with Alex going to achieve, exactly?

Finn was pulling back the covers on the bed when the bedroom door opened.

Alex padded into the room barefoot, his hair gleaming from his shower. He was using the bedroom next door to store his things and had changed into gray checkered pajama bottoms and a white T-shirt. He stopped when he saw Finn, his expression stiffening in the soft light of the lamps on the nightstands.

He glanced at Finn's bare chest and dark pajamas with a faint frown before looking pointedly at the side of the bed where Finn was standing.

"I usually sleep on the left."

"So do I," Finn said bluntly.

A muscle jumped in Alex's jawline. He raked a hand through his hair, something Finn was coming to realize the lawyer did when he was frustrated, and blew out a heavy sigh.

"Fine," Alex muttered testily. "Just keep to your side of the bed."

Finn raised an eyebrow. "What, scared I'm gonna jump you?"

Alex blinked, surprise flaring in his pale eyes for an instant.

Finn bit back a curse. *What the hell's gotten into me? Why am I taunting him?*

Alex recovered his composure and studied Finn with a scathing expression. "Newsflash. You're not my type."

"Well, that's a relief," Finn retorted.

Alex stormed around Finn, yanked the covers back, climbed in his side of the bed, and turned his light off.

Finn grimaced and rubbed the back of his neck before slowly doing the same.

Silence descended inside the room.

Finn stared at the glowing digits of the clock on his nightstand. He knew sleep would prove elusive tonight, just as it had every night for the last three years. He was still awake when Alex's breathing finally slowed into the steady pattern of a deep sleep.

Despite the distance that separated them, Finn was acutely conscious of the other man's body heat where he lay a short reach away.

Finn frowned as he recalled what Alex had said about Finn not being his type. He clenched his jaw and wondered if he was going crazy. Because, for one wild moment back there, he'd wanted to ask Alex what his type was.

CHAPTER FIVE

Damn it. I'm going stir crazy.

Alex closed his laptop and pinched the bridge of his nose. He gazed blindly at the darkening forest beyond the deck, the sound of running water from the nearby creek soothing his frayed nerves.

Bar Finn and his housekeeper, he hadn't seen anyone in over a week. And he wasn't sure if his interactions with Finn even counted as seeing the man. He was never there when Alex woke up and kept himself busy in his studio late into the night, so much so Alex didn't even know when he came to bed. Except for the odd meals they shared, they'd barely exchanged a handful of words since their wedding.

That had suited Alex fine for the first few days while he sorted out the mess Ryan had made of their firm in San Diego. Getting married wasn't the only life changing decision he'd come to when he'd agreed to come to Twilight Falls. He was dissolving his business in San Diego and using his savings to start afresh, here in his hometown. It would be on a trial basis for six months, after which he would need to decide whether to stay permanently in Twilight Falls or to return to San Diego. As luck would have it, one of Wyatt's friends was a local realtor and had emailed him particulars of places that had office space available to rent.

Alex let out a rueful sigh. He'd become too much of a city boy in the time he'd been in San Diego. It would be a while before he got used to the slower pace of life in Twilight Falls again.

Still, unlike a certain artist I know, it doesn't mean I have to live like a hermit. Time to get out of here and check out the scenery.

He put his stuff away, left a note for Finn, and rode the Triumph into town to grab an early dinner. He'd just set foot inside a quaint little Italian place when a familiar voice reached his ears.

"Well, if it isn't Alex Hancock."

Alex turned and spotted two men staring at him from where they sat sharing a meal near the back of the crowded room. He grimaced.

Here we go.

Hunter Thomson and Tristan Hart smiled at him faintly while he had a brief word with a waitress and made his way to their table.

"That look of fake surprise really doesn't suit you, Hunter," Alex muttered, taking the spare seat. "Wyatt tattled, didn't he?"

Hunter's smile widened. "Like a little girl. We played poker last night."

Alex turned to Tristan. "You thrashed their sorry asses?"

Tristan arched an eyebrow. "Always."

Alex felt some of the tension that had been weighing on him for the last month drain away. It had been a while since he'd last seen Hunter and Tristan. Alex stifled a sigh.

He was realizing once more just how much he'd missed the people he'd left behind when he'd moved to San Diego.

Wyatt, Hunter, and Tristan were but half of the group of close childhood friends Alex had grown up with in Twilight Falls. They'd met when they were five, after Alex's mom moved to town following his parents' divorce in Florida. Had their kindergarten teacher realized that the snot-nosed, brash kids who'd gotten into a fistfight on their first day of school would go on to become Twilight Falls' "Terrible Seven" and make the lives of their parents, teachers, and the town's sheriff hell over the decade and a half that followed, she would have done more than just scold them.

His friends' gazes locked on the gleaming band on Alex's ring finger.

"Is there something you need to share with us?" Hunter said, his expression sobering.

Alex rolled his wedding ring absent-mindedly around his finger. It felt just as strange now as it had on the day Finn had slipped it on his hand. True to form,

Izzy had picked perfectly-sized wedding bands for the both of them.

"How much did Wyatt tell you?"

"Just that you got yourself into some kind of trouble and had to come home," Tristan said in a serious voice.

Home, huh?

Alex looked out of the restaurant window and was surprised at how relaxed he felt being back in Twilight Falls, the antsy feeling he'd been experiencing all week fading fast.

He suspected his restlessness had more to do with the man he was sharing a roof with than with how isolated the estate was.

"So, you're gonna tell us who the lucky guy is?" Hunter said, distracting Alex from his troubled thoughts.

Alex met Hunter and Tristan's stares steadily. All of his friends knew he was gay. And he wasn't the only one in their group who was either.

"No one you know."

Hunter and Tristan picked up on his stiff tone. They shared a guarded glance while the waitress came over with Alex's water and took his order.

"Just how much trouble are you in, Alex?" Hunter said quietly.

Alex eyed the bottle of wine the two men were sharing. He was starting to wish he hadn't brought his bike into town just so he could have the drink he badly needed right now.

"Give or take, to the tune of half a million dollars," he finally admitted in a low voice.

Tristan choked on his wine.

Hunter's eyes widened. "Fuck me."

"No, thanks." Alex grimaced. "I don't think I could get hard for you."

A bark of laughter escaped Tristan as he wiped his mouth with his napkin. Several women in the room glanced over at their table, their admiring looks telling Alex they liked what they were seeing. Alex stifled a wry smile.

If only they knew.

"Sassy as always, I see," Tristan said, his eyes twinkling warmly.

"I'll have you know I'm a stud in the bedroom," Hunter stated with an arrogant half-smile.

"Sure you are," Alex drawled, enjoying their banter. "The answer's still no, studman."

Tristan chuckled.

Hunter leaned forward, elbows on the table and expression turning conspiratorial. "So, you're sleeping with this guy?"

Alex rolled his eyes hard at his friends. "What is this, the high-school locker room?"

The pair of inquisitive gazes opposite him did not waver.

Christ, these two are worse than the Spanish Inquisition.

"We're sleeping in the same bed," Alex admitted grudgingly. "It's part of the contract."

Hunter sucked in air.

Tristan's smile faded. "Contract?" His tone turned hard. "So, this is some kind of arranged gig? This guy paid you to marry him?"

Alex hushed him and looked around nervously.

No one appeared to have overheard them.

He chewed the inside of his cheek as he studied his two friends. He couldn't exactly deny that that was precisely what had happened.

"Doesn't sound to me like you're sleeping *with* him though," Hunter said curiously. "I take it that means sex isn't part of the deal?"

"It isn't," Alex murmured. "Izzy would never have proposed this arrangement to me otherwise."

Tristan groaned. "Christ, Izzy's involved in this?"

Hunter's expression grew pained. "I should have guessed. That woman is a born trouble maker."

"Don't be hard on her," Alex protested. "She really bailed me out this time." He hesitated. "Besides, Finn's straight, so you both can stop worrying about me."

Alex mulled over what he'd said to Hunter and Tristan as he rode his Triumph back up the mountain later that night. Finn *was* straight, so however attractive Alex found him, nothing was ever going to happen between them.

And the sooner I accept that fact, the better.

The house was dark when Alex crested the rise in the driveway.

That's strange. Finn must have gone to bed early.

Alex rode down to the building and let himself inside. He was halfway to the stairs when a sound reached him. It had come from the direction of Finn's studio.

Oh. He's still up.

Alex hesitated, wondering whether he should go say

hi. A grimace twisted his lips. He doubted Finn wanted his company, otherwise he wouldn't be doing his damnedest to avoid him.

Alex was about to make his way to their bedroom when a loud crash echoed from the other end of the house.

CHAPTER SIX

ALEX STARTLED. HE TURNED AND BOLTED TOWARD Finn's studio, fear sending his pulse into the stratosphere. He reached the end of the corridor, yanked the studio door open, and dashed inside the giant glass box, only to stumble to an abrupt halt.

Finn stood barefoot with his back to him in the middle of the room, the smashed pieces of a sculpture on the floor around him.

Alex stepped toward him. "Hey, are you—"

His words died in his throat when Finn turned to face him.

The artist was holding a half empty bottle of whiskey casually in one hand. But it wasn't the fact that he looked thoroughly wasted that stunned Alex.

Instead, it was the tortured expression on the other man's face and the self-hatred filling his eyes that made Alex draw a sharp breath. Alex glanced around and noted the mess inside the studio.

It looked like a storm had swept over the place.

What the hell happened here?

He masked the nervous tension thrumming through him and met Finn's stare.

"Did you do that?" Alex indicated the broken sculpture.

Finn brought the bottle of whiskey to his lips in a nonchalant gesture and swallowed a mouthful of liquor, his moody gaze focused unblinkingly on Alex.

"What does it matter?"

Alex frowned. It was becoming clear to him that whatever demons possessed Finn West had taken hold of him tonight and he'd decided to drown himself in alcohol to forget them.

"You're drunk."

A dispassionate chuckle left Finn's lips. "Yeah, I am. What is it to you?" He arched an eyebrow, his expression disparaging. "You're not my wife."

Anger flashed through Alex. He raised his chin challengingly.

"No, I'm not your wife," he retorted. "Quite frankly, I don't think she'd be thrilled at your behavior if she were standing here right now."

Finn went deathly still. His eyes slowly darkened with fury.

Alex bit his lip. *Shit. That was obviously too close to home.*

Finn took a step toward him. Alex moved back reflexively.

Finn narrowed his eyes and closed the distance between them in a flash.

Alex was steeling himself for a punch when Finn

grabbed his shoulder and walked him back forcefully to the closest wall. Alex gasped as he found himself trapped between a thick sheet of glass and the man towering over him.

Finn placed the bottle of whiskey on a nearby worktop and took hold of Alex's face in his callused hands. Goosebumps blasted across Alex's skin at Finn's heated touch. He gripped Finn's wrists to wrench his arms away and was surprised at the other man's strength when the latter resisted him.

"You're not my wife," Finn repeated, slurring his words slightly.

Alex swallowed, hyperaware of the tall, masculine body close to his. He could smell Finn's cologne above the reek of whiskey on the other man's breath.

Damn. This is bad.

Not seeing Finn for the last week had made Alex forget what a powerful impact the man he'd married could have on him this close up.

"No," Alex blurted out. "I'm your husband."

Finn stiffened at Alex's retort. He lowered his gaze.

Alex blinked. *Wait, is he looking at—*

"Funny," Finn murmured. He rubbed a slow thumb across Alex's lower lip.

Alex's thoughts scattered to the four winds. His senses arrowed in on the shocking feeling of Finn's intimate caress. He met Finn's gaze, alarmed, and felt his stomach plummet.

Finn's eyes were feverish, dark pools threatening to swallow Alex in whatever madness had taken hold of him.

"You sure don't act like my husband." With that, Finn lowered his head and took Alex's mouth in a savage kiss.

Alex gasped. *What the—*

Finn took advantage of Alex's parted lips and delved inside his mouth. Alex's cock twitched. He made a small sound as Finn pushed a muscular thigh between his legs, spreading him wide open.

This isn't happening! Why is he—

Heat ignited in Alex's veins when Finn pressed into him, molding their bodies together just as he had their mouths, his hot gaze boring relentlessly into Alex's dazed stare. Alex ignored the voice at the back of his head screaming that this was a bad idea and gave in to temptation. Eyes fluttering closed, he surrendered himself to Finn's kiss and touch.

A groan of approval echoed from Finn when he sensed Alex's submission. He sucked on Alex's lips and nipped Alex's tongue with his teeth before wrapping his own hot flesh around Alex's in a seductive move that had Alex weak at the knees.

Desire swept over Alex, making him dizzy. He let go of Finn's wrists and grabbed the back of Finn's head, his fingers stabbing urgently through Finn's thick hair. A feral sound rumbled out of Finn's chest at Alex's desperate touch. The kiss went from savage, to slow and sultry.

Alex's dick hardened in an instant.

Oh God.

Finn was exploring his lips and mouth as if he was

the finest dish he'd ever tasted, his breaths heavy and his touch fierce on Alex's face.

Alex moaned, powerless to stop his hips from punching forward and pressing his hot, hard length into Finn's groin. It had been so long since he'd had sex and he knew he was close to self-combusting in the arms of the man who was devouring him as if his life depended on it.

He blinked when something stiff nudged his thigh.

The man, who by the feel of the erection digging into Alex, was just as aroused as he was.

This startling realization had barely sunk into Alex's dazed mind when Finn suddenly let go of his mouth. Alex grunted as the other man leaned heavily into him, pushing him against the glass wall. Finn's head drooped into the crook of Alex's neck, his hot breath sending a shiver racing through Alex.

"Finn?" Alex mumbled. A soft snore reached his ears. He stared at the sleeping man in his arms, his heart thundering against his ribs and his dick doing painful press-ups behind his zipper. "Are you kidding me?!"

CHAPTER SEVEN

Light stabbed through Finn's eyelids. He flinched and shielded his eyes with a hand. Blinding pain gripped his temples in the next instant. It was followed by a wave of nausea. Finn groaned and lay still, sweat beading his forehead while he fought down the urge to throw up. It was a moment before he managed a shaky breath and carefully blinked his eyes open.

Sun drenched trees filled his vision. Finn winced at the brightness and looked around slowly, the headache now a physical presence drilling through his skull.

He was lying on a couch in the living room. Someone, Alex presumably, had laid a blanket over him. Finn's gaze found the glass of water on the coffee table in front of him.

The last thing he remembered was grabbing a bottle of whiskey from the liquor cabinet in the dining room and heading inside his studio. Guilt stabbed through him. It was a habit he had fallen into lately: drinking to forget the past.

The soft sound of footsteps reached him just as he sat up. Finn looked around and groaned when the sudden movement made his head throb alarmingly.

Alex was crossing the floor from the direction of the kitchen, two steaming cups in hand. He was barefoot and dressed in ripped jeans and a T-shirt, his wet hair catching the sunlight.

The smell of freshly brewed coffee struck Finn's nose. His stomach rumbled. For some reason, finding Alex's note last night had made him lose his appetite and he'd ended up not having dinner.

Well I did, kinda. It was a liquid one.

Alex wordlessly offered him one of the cups.

"Thanks," Finn murmured.

Alex turned and took a seat in the armchair opposite the couch. Finn studied him curiously while he took a cautious sip of his coffee. Alex was looking at him with a strange expression. Finn blinked.

He almost looks...angry.

"How's your head?" Alex asked in a conversational tone.

Finn grimaced. "Terrible."

A hard smile curved Alex's lips. "Good."

Finn stared. "That's a pretty shitty thing to say to someone who has a hangover."

Alex leaned back in the armchair, crossed his right leg atop his left knee, and took a leisurely sip of his coffee. "Yeah, well, it's payback for last night."

Finn frowned. "What do you mean?"

Alex smiled humorlessly. "I mean it's payback for having to drag your sorry, unconscious ass out of your studio all the way here just so you wouldn't sleep on a cold stone floor."

Something in Alex's eyes made Finn's stomach flutter with a bout of nervousness. Though he couldn't recollect what exactly had happened last night, he couldn't shake the feeling that he'd said or done something to piss Alex off.

"I'm sorry," Finn murmured. "The last thing I remember is heading in there with a bottle of whiskey." He made a face. "I didn't realize I was so drunk."

Surprise flashed in Alex's eyes for a moment, as if he hadn't expected the apology. Remorse twisted through Finn once more.

Shit. He really thinks I'm an asshole, doesn't he? Finn fought back a sigh. *Well, considering how I've been avoiding him lately, I can't really blame him.*

"So, you're saying you have no recollection of what you did?"

Finn's knuckles whitened on his drink at Alex's accusing tone. "What—" He paused and swallowed uneasily. Something told him he didn't want to hear what Alex was going to say next. "What did I do?"

Alex watched him for a silent moment. "You smashed one of your sculptures."

Finn winced. "I did?"

"Yeah. It was the one you were working on."

"Oh." Embarrassment flared through Finn. He rubbed the back of his neck awkwardly. "I've been stuck on that piece for a while. It's probably a good thing I broke it. I can start over again."

Alex gazed at him steadily. "You also made a mess of the rest of your studio."

Finn sighed. "Nothing too irreversible, I hope?"

Alex shook his head.

Relief flooded Finn. "Was that all?"

"No. That was just the opening act."

Tension gripped Finn all over again.

"The humdinger was when you pushed me against the wall and kissed me," Alex said. "Very thoroughly, I might add."

A ringing noise started in Finn's ears. He stared unblinkingly at Alex above the sound of blood suddenly rushing through his head, unsure if he'd just heard the shocking words the other man had just uttered.

"What did you just say?" Finn mumbled.

"I said you kissed me!" Alex snapped. "Forcefully."

"That's impossible!" Finn blurted out. "I'm—I'm not gay!"

Alex's eyes turned a stormy blue. "Your erection said otherwise."

The room shifted dizzyingly around Finn. His heartbeat echoed loudly in his ears as he gazed at the man opposite him. The man whose accusing words had just turned his entire world upside down.

"My—my erection?" he said hoarsely.

A frown wrinkled Alex's brow. "Jesus, you've gone as pale as a ghost. There's no need to look so fucking disgusted." He uncrossed his legs and put his cup on the side table next to him with a thunk. "So, you kissed a guy and got hard," he snorted. "It's not the end of the world."

"I'm impotent," Finn said numbly.

❧

ALEX WENT STILL AS FINN'S CONFESSION REVERBERATED around the lounge.

"What?" he said in a stunned voice.

"I'm impotent," the man opposite him repeated.

Finn's cup trembled in his grip. He put it on the floor next to him and clasped his knees to stop the tremors, the tormented expression from last night pasted across his face once more.

"I—" Finn stopped and closed his eyes briefly, a muscle dancing in his cheek. "I can't get hard. Catherine and I—" He rubbed a hand across his face. "We barely had a sex life. We slept in the same bed but I could never satisfy her. Sexually."

Alex stared. He could tell Finn was being deadly serious. No one could look so racked with shame and guilt and be faking it.

Something's not right here. He was definitely aroused last night.

"Were you diagnosed as impotent?" Alex said, intrigued.

"I didn't need to be," Finn replied awkwardly. "I was in love with Catherine. Had been for a long time. We were childhood sweethearts." A nostalgic expression danced across his face. "We got married pretty young."

Alex had deliberately not quizzed Izzy about Finn's

past beyond what she'd revealed to him on their wedding day. As far as he was concerned, Finn's previous marriage was none of his business.

But what had happened in the studio last night had changed Alex's feelings on the matter. However much Finn wanted to deny it, he'd kissed and responded to Alex.

"When did you realize you were impotent?" Alex asked curiously.

Color stained Finn's cheekbones at the direct question. He hesitated.

"On our wedding night. We'd kissed and fooled around when we were dating, but we'd both decided to wait until we got married to have sex."

Alex pursed his lips. "That's pretty old-fashioned in this day and age."

Finn remained silent.

Alex rested his elbows on his knees, propped his chin on the back of his knuckles, and studied Finn thoughtfully.

Finn practically squirmed where he sat under Alex's intent stare.

"And you've never gotten hard?" Alex said, aware he was grilling Finn as he were a witness on the stand. "For anyone else?"

"There's never been anyone else," Finn admitted.

Alex arched an eyebrow. "What about handjobs?"

Finn's eyes rounded. "We're not having this conversation!" he spluttered.

Alex smiled faintly. "I'm going to choose to interpret that as a yes."

Finn scowled, grabbed the glass of water by his feet, and gulped it down in one go.

A filthy vision danced through Alex's mind as he watched Finn's Adam's apple bob up and down. He swallowed a groan.

Now's really not the time to be getting turned on, Hancock.

Finn finished his drink and wiped his mouth with the back of his hand, oblivious to Alex's dirty musings.

"You can interpret it as you like," he declared haughtily. "Now, if you don't mind, I'm going to go have a shower."

Alex's smile widened as he watched Finn head up the stairs.

Despite Finn's painful confession just now, he couldn't help but feel a small buzz of excitement. Life with Finn West was about to get interesting. Because, whether Finn liked it or not, he had most definitely been aroused last night.

Besides, no one can kiss like that and not mean it.

CHAPTER EIGHT

FINN FROWNED AT THE BLOCK OF CLAY ON THE modeling table in front of him. It had been two days since he'd put the blasted thing there and he was still no further along on what he wanted to do with it. He rubbed a hand across the back of his neck and sighed for what felt like the tenth time that morning.

He knew damn well the reason why he couldn't concentrate. The cause of his distraction was five foot nine, had blond hair, blue eyes, and a perfectly-shaped, sassy mouth. Finn grimaced.

A mouth I apparently kissed. Thoroughly, according to him.

His ears warmed at that thought. He still couldn't believe that he'd pushed Alex against the wall and practically attacked him. He'd never done anything like that to anyone in his life, including Catherine.

A bittersweet feeling washed over Finn as he looked over at the picture on the shelf, the only one he'd kept of the two of them after her death.

He had truly loved Catherine. And she had been head over heels in love with him too. He knew she'd been devastated when he couldn't consummate their marriage on their very first night together. Although they'd eventually managed to have sex after a fashion, it wasn't the way she'd wanted to be with him, physically. He'd been able to pleasure Catherine with his hands and mouth, but never with his body.

Catherine had never blamed him for the fact that he was impotent. After trying to get him to see a specialist for the first few years of their marriage, she had quietly resigned herself to his condition, just as he had. As far as Finn had been concerned, not being able to have sex with the woman he loved wasn't something that could be cured.

It was when he'd finally agreed to her wish to get pregnant and accompanied her on one of her appointments to a private IVF clinic in L.A. that they'd discovered she had cancer. Finn would never forget that awful day for as long as he lived. The despair he'd felt at the knowledge that he would soon lose Catherine. Her own heartrending anguish at not being able to bear them a child. The irrevocable fact that had he agreed to her demand sooner, she might have been diagnosed earlier.

Still, Catherine had never complained. Not once. Not even at the very end of her long illness. That, above everything else, was what Finn hated himself the most for.

That Catherine had never allowed herself to openly mourn. To grieve their abject marriage and his failure as her husband. To cry over the knowledge that she would never get pregnant.

Finn frowned.

Alex must be wrong. There's no way I could have become aroused just from kissing him. Not when I couldn't get hard for my own wife.

Unfortunately, there was only one way to test the truth of Alex's statement. And that was to kiss him again.

Finn clenched his jaw. The thing was, kissing Alex was all he'd been able to think about since the morning he'd made his agonizing disclosure to the man about the state of his marriage to Catherine. Luckily for him, the lawyer had been busy visiting office rentals in town for the last two days and was rarely at home. Which meant he probably hadn't noticed how Finn had been surreptitiously looking at his lips and wondering what they would feel like under his.

"I bet they're soft," Finn mumbled to himself.

He groaned. *Jesus, I can't believe I just said that out loud!*

"You bet what's soft?" someone said behind him.

Finn startled and turned around so fast he almost fell off his stool.

Izzy blinked at him from where she stood in the doorway of the studio.

Finn let out an exasperated sigh. "Have you heard of knocking?"

"I did." Izzy strolled inside the room, a frown wrinkling her brow. "What's the matter? You look, I don't know—" she waved a vague hand in the air, "kinda distracted."

"It's nothing," Finn muttered. "Why are you here?"

"We had a meeting." Izzy dropped her bag on a worktop and eyed him suspiciously. "Seriously, what's wrong? You never forget our appointments."

"Like I said, it's nothing," Finn repeated, trying hard not to let the guilt he was feeling color his voice. He couldn't very well tell Izzy that he'd spent the last two days fantasizing about kissing one of her closest friends. "I'm sorry, it completely slipped my mind. Give me a minute and I'll get the stuff ready."

Izzy glanced at the virgin block of clay on the modeling table. "I thought you were already working on something."

"I was. It didn't pan out."

Izzy raised an eyebrow. "That's unusual."

"Blame it on a bad week," Finn said in a deliberately evasive tone. *And a guy with blue eyes and a mouth I really want to kiss.*

He blinked at that sudden illicit thought.

Wait. Am I thinking of kissing him because I want to see if he was right or because I...I want to?!

"Why don't I make us some coffee?" Izzy suggested, oblivious to the startling question blazing through Finn's mind.

Finn nodded, grateful for the interruption. Remorse filled him when he noted the anxious light in Izzy's eyes.

I'm just tired. There's no way I want *to kiss Alex. He might be gay, but I'm definitely not.*

CHAPTER NINE

Alex parked his Triumph next to Finn's Jeep and studied the red Mini on the drive with a faint frown. He hadn't realized Izzy was coming to the house today.

A rumble of conversation reached him when he entered the vestibule. Izzy's bubbly laughter echoed from the direction of the kitchen. Alex put his bag down and followed the sound. He slowed to a stop just inside the doorway of the kitchen.

Finn and Izzy stood at the modern black range on the other side of the island. They had their backs to him and were talking in relaxed voices while they stirred a couple of steaming pans.

Something twisted inside Alex's chest as he gazed at them.

They look like a couple.

He must have made a noise for Izzy turned and spotted him.

"Hey, hot stuff." She smiled, unaware of the green-eyed monster that had just stirred inside him.

"Guess what? I taught Finn how to make my mamma's spaghetti bolognaise. You two will no longer starve like the sorry little lambs that you are."

Alex's stomach rumbled as his nose finally registered the delicious smells wafting through the room.

"Alex's a pretty good cook." Finn studied Alex with an inscrutable expression. "And our housekeeper's been making some of our meals."

"No one beats my Kung Pao chicken," Alex said lightly. He accepted the glass of champagne Izzy poured him and leaned against a countertop. "So, what's the occasion?" He indicated the open bottle on the island with a curious tilt of his head.

Izzy's face lit up with excitement. "Finn has an art exhibition coming up in L.A. It's in two months. The whole town's already talking about it!"

Finn grimaced. "Calling the L.A. art world the whole town is a bit of an exaggeration, Izz."

Alex noted the affectionate diminutive with another twinge. He masked a frown of irritation at the resentment that had surged through him.

Jesus, I'm acting as if he's cheating on me or something!

"Nonsense," Izzy said dismissively. "The turnout is gonna be awesome. I'm already putting the guest list together. And we'll even have an A-list movie star spearheading the whole show!"

Finn raised his eyebrows. "An A-list movie star?"

Alex sighed when he observed the devilish glint in Izzy's eyes. "Let me guess. You twisted Carter's arm?"

Finn looked between the two of them, puzzled. "Who's Carter?"

"Carter Wilson." Alex took a sip of his drink. "He's a childhood friend of ours."

Finn's eyes widened. "*The* Carter Wilson? As in the guy who's been headlining most of the blockbuster movies these past three years? The actor who just won an Oscar for his role in that WWII film that had all the critics in tears?"

"The very one." Izzy arched an eyebrow, her expression dry. "Jeez, Finn, I didn't think you'd know who he was."

Finn rolled his eyes. "I'm not a complete Luddite."

Izzy grinned. "Anyhow, Carter owes me one."

Alex narrowed his eyes at her accusingly. "You mean, you blackmailed him, didn't you?"

Izzy beamed, her expression angelic.

"What do you mean?" Finn muttered.

"Izzy sneaked into the boys' locker room when we were in high school and took a picture of Carter's naked ass," Alex explained in a disgruntled tone. "She's been holding that picture over his head ever since that day."

Finn looked appropriately shocked. "That's terrible!"

"Ah, it's all in jest," Izzy protested with a wave of her hand. "Besides, Carter knows it's an empty threat. Mostly." A saucy grin curved her lips. "And, let's face it, the guy's exposed more than just his ass on the big screen since."

Alex chuckled while Finn shook his head in exasperation.

Dinner ended up being a fun affair despite Alex's earlier misgivings. Having Izzy there as a buffer meant he and Finn could have a normal conversation again.

Alex knew the incident in the studio was still weighing on Finn's mind. Although he'd wanted nothing more than to test his growing theory about Finn's sexuality, he'd deliberately stayed out of the artist's way since the morning he'd told him about their kiss and had kept himself busy finalizing the rental agreement of his new office in town. As luck would have it, the place he'd chosen was around the corner from Hunter's sports apparel shop and he'd gone out with his friend a couple of times for coffee and lunch to keep himself distracted.

Izzy picked up her bag an hour later and made to leave.

"Can I leave you boys to take care of the washing up? I told Wyatt I'd be home before midnight."

"Sure thing," Alex murmured. The champagne had melted his tension away and he was feeling mellow. He patted his stomach. "Once we can move, that is. Your mamma's spaghetti bolognese is as lethal as I remember it being. I very rarely have third helpings of anything."

"Yup," Finn concurred, looking similarly full.

The artist had abstained from having more than one glass of champagne with his food. Alex had also noticed that the bottles of whiskey previously housed in the liquor cabinet had ended up in the recycling when he'd thrown an empty carton of milk in there that morning.

He had to admit to having mixed feelings on the subject.

On the one hand, it was a good move on Finn's part to stop drinking. Alex suspected the artist had indulged in more than his fair share of that particular activity since his wife's death. On the other hand, it seemed to him that Finn was determined for there not to be a repeat of that night in his studio.

"See you two studs soon!" Izzy called out as she headed out of the house.

The door thudded closed behind her.

"Shall we?" Alex said after a short silence. He rose and started clearing the table. Finn followed suit.

Alex headed into the kitchen and began stacking the dishwasher. Finn came up behind him. Alex turned to take the next set of dirty dishes off him and stiffened.

Finn was standing very close to him.

"Hmm," Alex mumbled, startled by the artist's sudden proximity.

"I want to do it again," Finn said in a low voice.

Alex blinked at him, mystified. "Do what again?"

A muscle twitched in Finn's jawline. Alex realized Finn was clutching the plates in his hands as if they were a lifeline. Finn's gaze dropped to Alex's mouth. Alex's pulse jumped.

"Kiss you," Finn admitted between clenched teeth.

"What?" Alex breathed.

Finn met Alex's shocked stare.

Alex swallowed. He could tell an inner battle was raging inside Finn from the way the artist's eyes had darkened. Finn put the plates on the countertop, his movements slow and deliberate.

"I said I want to kiss you again. To see if you were right about that night."

Taut silence filled the kitchen.

"Okay," Alex said quietly. He stared at Finn, heart thumping and palms sweaty with sudden nervous anticipation.

Finn hesitated, as if unsure what to do next.

Alex licked his dry lips. "Why don't I get us started?"

He raised his fingers to Finn's face.

A shudder shook Finn at Alex's touch; he closed his eyes, his expression almost pained. Alex's stomach clenched, certain it was disgust Finn was experiencing. He was about to lower his hands and call it a night when Finn opened his eyes once more.

Alex's breath caught in his throat.

He could see it now. Finn's desire to kiss him. Though Finn seemed to be fighting his instincts and looked both angry and conflicted, the expression blazing out of his dark gaze told Alex he wanted this badly.

Alex threw caution to the wind, tugged Finn's head down, and pressed their mouths together.

SOFT. THAT WAS FINN'S FIRST IMPRESSION OF ALEX'S lips. And hot. So hot, they threatened to scorch him.

Alex's eyes shone a bright blue as he angled his head and carefully molded their mouths together. Finn stilled, absorbing it all. The way Alex felt against him. The hint of color staining his cheekbones. His smell and his body heat.

Something told Finn he needed to burn the details of this kiss in his memory.

He stiffened when he felt Alex's tongue probing his lips. He parted them and let Alex in, curious as to how it would feel to have another man inside his mouth.

Alex's eyes fluttered closed. A bewildering sense of loss swept over Finn when he could no longer peer into the heated blue gaze beneath him.

Alex deepened their kiss.

Finn blinked. *Damn. He's good.*

He froze when their tongues finally met, Alex's wrapping softly around his, as if he was scared Finn would bolt. Goosebumps exploded across Finn's skin. He shuddered, his body temperature shooting up so fast his head spun.

Alex made a low hungry sound and sucked on Finn's tongue.

Finn grabbed Alex's wrists and wrenched their mouths apart.

They stared at each other in the fraught silence, their breaths coming hard and fast. Alex's pulse raced under Finn's fingertips. Finn swallowed.

It matched his own pounding heart.

Something that looked very much like hurt washed across Alex's face.

"Looks like you can only do this when you're

drunk, huh?" he mumbled, the corners of his mouth twisting in a self-deprecating half-smile.

Finn shook his head, too overcome with emotion to speak.

"You're wrong," he whispered, more to himself than to Alex.

Confusion replaced the disappointment in Alex's eyes.

"You're wrong," Finn repeated firmly, finally acknowledging what his mind and body were telling him.

He lowered his head and kissed Alex.

Alex went deathly still. Finn licked the lawyer's lower lip, bit down gently on the plump, wet flesh, and tugged it between his teeth. Alex inhaled sharply. Finn slowly sucked and laved the soft wound he'd just made. Alex's eyes turned indigo with desire. Finn's pulse spiked.

Shit.

He crowded Alex against the counter and delved hungrily past Alex's lips.

Alex's soft sigh of surrender fluttered across Finn's tongue as he started exploring the heated depths of the lawyer's mouth. He entwined his arms around Finn's neck and clung on to him for dear life, as if his legs could no longer support his own weight.

Finn groaned when his tongue met Alex's. Alex tasted of coffee and champagne and more. He wrapped their flesh together over and over again, dizzy at how incredible it all felt. Alex's lips. His mouth. His trembling, hot, eager tongue. His strong, hard body pressed intimately against Finn's frame.

By the time he lifted his mouth from Alex's and ended their blistering kiss, Finn knew his life would never be the same again. Because he could no longer deny what was happening. What was between them. What had been there, simmering in the background, probably since the very first day they met.

Desire. Passion. Lust.

Finn could see all of it in Alex's own heated gaze as the lawyer blinked his glazed eyes open.

Alex bit his swollen lower lip, his cheeks dark with color. "Well, I think we can safely conclude that you're not impotent."

A shaky chuckle escaped Finn. He touched his forehead to Alex's, his erection pressing uncomfortably against the zipper of his jeans.

"You can say that again," he mumbled.

CHAPTER TEN

ALEX STIRRED AND OPENED HIS EYES. HE BLINKED AT THE daylight streaming inside the room. Disappointment pierced him when he saw the empty bed next to him. It faded at the sound of running water coming from the adjacent bathroom.

Alex pressed the heels of his hands to his eyes and groaned, his blood heating up as a vision of Finn naked in the shower blazed across his mind.

It had been late when they'd retired to their bedroom last night. Nothing more had happened following their kiss in the kitchen. Finn's realization that he was not impotent and that his body had responded to a man's touch and kiss was such a staggering, life changing event for the artist that both men had consciously made the decision not to pursue where it could lead.

"I need some time to process this," Finn had admitted, his expression a gut-wrenching mix of confusion and doubt.

"I know," Alex had murmured in return. "It's not every day you realize you might be gay."

Something had shifted in Finn's eyes at Alex's words. "Do you really think that? That I'm gay?"

Alex had given this question the just consideration it deserved. "The fact that you loved your wife means you might be bisexual."

Finn had gone quiet for a moment. "Thank you," he'd mumbled finally.

Alex had gazed at him, puzzled. "For what?"

Finn's lips had lifted in a sad smile. "For not denying that what I felt for Catherine—for my wife, was real."

Alex had wanted to touch Finn then. He'd wanted to take him in his arms and hold him. To kiss him and allay his fears. To tell him that what he was feeling was not wrong. That it was okay for him to be attracted to another man. Instead, he'd smiled at Finn and told him that it was nothing.

Falling asleep after everything that had happened between them had proven an almost impossible task. Though they'd resolved not to go beyond a kiss, being so close to Finn and not being able to touch him had been an exercise in sheer torture for Alex. He'd gotten used to Finn's body heat and physical presence in the two weeks they'd been sharing a bed, but last night had been different.

Alex had been conscious of every breath, every move, every soft sound Finn had made as he lay next to him. Knowing that all he had to do was reach across the bed and touch Finn had gotten Alex so hard he'd spent a good part of the night in considerable discomfort.

The bathroom door opened. Alex lowered his hands from his face in time to see Finn emerge in a cloud of steam. He swallowed, his mouth suddenly dry.

Finn was naked but for a towel wrapped around his hips. Water gleamed in his hair and formed a sheen on his chest and strong, toned legs.

Alex watched, mesmerized, as a stray droplet fell from Finn's temple and ran down his six-pack before disappearing behind the towel. He dug his nails into his palms and resisted the urge to climb out of bed, go over to Finn, and lick the path it had taken.

"Stop that," Finn admonished.

Alex blinked. "Stop what?"

"Stop looking at me like you want to eat me," Finn said, his ears reddening.

"I was thinking of licking you all over first, actually," Alex confessed unashamedly.

Finn's eyes widened. "Shit."

Alex's gaze dropped to Finn's towel. There was definite tenting going on. He grinned. "Someone's happy to see me."

Finn groaned and stormed back into the bathroom.

Alex laughed.

He's going to be the death of me.

Finn stared at Alex where he sat opposite him.

Three days had passed since their kiss.

They were having breakfast on the veranda next to the kitchen. Alex was buttering his toast and eating it with every ounce of enjoyment.

This innocent activity would normally not have bothered Finn.

Except Alex was savoring his food as if it were the most sinfully delicious thing that had ever passed his lips. And the sight was slowly driving Finn out of his mind with desire.

A trail of warm butter oozed onto Alex's hand. Alex ducked his head and licked the golden mess. Finn bit back a curse when Alex slowly sucked his fingers into his mouth one at a time, giving them a thorough cleaning with his clever tongue.

Alex let go of his hand, his lips glistening wetly. "Is something wrong?"

Finn knew better than to trust the lawyer's innocent voice. "Are you deliberately trying to seduce me?"

Alex raised his eyebrows. "I don't know what you mean." His blue eyes sparkled with mischief. "Besides, if I were truly trying to seduce you, I would have chosen something more exciting than bread and butter."

Finn stifled a sigh at the filthy thoughts still filling his mind.

Bread and butter are working just fine.

"Like, say, strawberries and cream." Alex leaned back in his chair, leveled a steady stare at Finn, and brought his cup to his lips.

Finn's dirty musings reached new heights as he

watched Alex's Adam's apple bob up and down with a sip of coffee.

Shit. Is that what he'd look like if he swallowed my—

Finn clenched his jaw and suppressed the torrid image blazing across his vision. Considering he'd told Alex he needed time to sort out his feelings about their kiss, he could hardly tell him that he'd been busy fantasizing about what else they could do for the last three days.

"Strawberries and cream, huh?" he mumbled to mask his chagrin.

"Yup." Alex smiled faintly. "First, I'd take a strawberry in my fingers and dip it in cream until it was completely coated."

Finn felt a stirring in his groin at the sinful image Alex was painting.

"Then I would eat it," Alex continued, his voice dropping an octave. "Real slow. I would pop it between my lips, sink my teeth into that pink, juicy flesh, and lick all that delicious, thick, cream with my tongue until—"

Finn made a strangled sound, the stirring now a painful, throbbing ache between his thighs. An ache he very much wanted the man opposite him to assuage with those filthy lips of his.

"Are you okay?" Alex drawled.

Finn wasn't fooled by Alex's casual tone. He could tell from Alex's slightly flushed cheeks and the way his breathing had sped up that he was as aroused as Finn was right now.

"No, I'm not okay," Finn said between gritted teeth.

"I'm hard and I want to come over there and get you to do something about it."

"Like what?"

Finn hesitated at Alex's question.

"What do you want me to do, Finn?" Alex's expression turned serious.

Though Finn knew exactly what he yearned for Alex to do to him, saying the words loud meant entering unknown territory. And he wasn't sure he was ready to take that leap yet.

Alex observed Finn with an enigmatic expression.

"Why don't you think about it some more?" The lawyer rose to his feet. "I'm going out for the day."

"When will you be back?" Finn said before he could stop himself. He bit his lip, aware of how needy he'd sounded.

Alex's soft smile told Finn he'd guessed his thoughts. "I'll be back in the afternoon. We can talk then."

CHAPTER ELEVEN

ALEX PULLED INTO A BAY RESERVED FOR MOTORCYCLES, switched his engine off, and removed his helmet. He ran a hand through his hair before nervously eyeing the pretty, rambling, two-story building perched on a gentle slope overlooking Twilight Falls River.

With its red shingle roof, pale walls, and a split-level wrap around terrace dotted with comfortable deck chairs and flowerpots, the Sunrise Care Home was as picturesque as its stunning surroundings. Which made the butterflies churning Alex's stomach all the more out of place. He clenched his jaw.

This is way overdue. Just get your shit together and do this, Hancock.

The rumble of a powerful engine reached Alex's ears, distracting him. He looked around. A black Harley flitted into view between the trees to the north. Alex's heart sank when it came around the corner.

Great. Just great.

The Harley stormed up the drive and curved

around Alex's Triumph before stopping a few feet away. Alex watched grimly as the last man he wanted to see right now shut down the engine and took off his helmet.

Drake Jackson shook out his long, brown hair and pinned Alex with an intense blue stare. "Hi."

Alex's pulse fluttered as he gazed at the man he'd given his virginity to fourteen years ago. Drake was one of Twilight Falls' "Terrible Seven," along with Wyatt, Tristan, Hunter, and Carter.

It wasn't until they'd reached their teens that Alex had started to become conscious of Drake as more than just a childhood friend. Drake was the first one of them whose body had matured with puberty, shooting up to over six feet in one summer and developing a lean, muscled physique that had all the girls in high school fawning over him.

In truth, Alex had had a crush on Drake long before that.

It happened on the night of his sixteenth birthday. After consuming one too many of the beers Tristan and Carter had sneaked from their old men's stash, Alex had finally worked up the courage to tell Drake that he liked him, after the others had fallen asleep in his living room. He'd known it was a stupid thing to do, what with the rest of their friends within earshot and the rumors that Drake had slept with several girls in their class and even an older woman at the forefront of his mind.

To his utter shock, Drake had not only accepted his feelings but had taken Alex up to his bedroom in the attic and had sex with him. Though their first time together had been more painful than gratifying for Alex, he'd gone back to Drake time and time again after that night, eager to explore his burgeoning sexuality and those tantalizing bolts of pleasure he'd experienced while Drake was inside him.

Sex between them had gotten hot pretty fast and it wasn't long before Alex was drowning in the ecstasy he found in Drake's arms. They'd made love whenever and wherever they could, often stealing short, intense moments in Drake's parents' garage or in the woods behind Alex's house. Being taken by Drake from behind while kneeling on all fours on the forest floor, his fingers curling into crisp woodland grass and his head thrown back to a boundless blue sky as he moaned and grunted and shouted in pleasure while Drake thrust hard and fast and deep inside him was still one of the lasting memories of Alex's sixteenth summer.

But it became rapidly clear to Alex that Drake wanted a physical relationship rather an emotional one. Drake came from an even more broken family than Alex's and had protected his heart jealously ever since Alex had known him. Though Alex knew Drake loved him as a childhood friend, having Drake fall in love with him was a whole other matter.

They'd broken up the next summer, eight months before the accident happened.

"So, you're going in or what?" Drake arched an eyebrow and cocked his head at the care home.

Alex hesitated. "To be honest, I'm scared shitless to walk in there," he admitted bluntly.

Drake watched him for a moment. "It wasn't your fault, Alex," he finally said, his voice softer than Alex recalled it being. "You know that, right? Miles would never blame you for what happened that night. Neither does Elaine." He paused. "None of us do."

Alex swallowed, the guilt that had plagued him for the last twelve years washing over him all over again and bringing with it a sharp pang of pain and regret.

"I was the one driving," he said bitterly.

Drake sighed. "And the other guy was twice over the drink driving limit."

"If I'd swerved the other way—" Alex mumbled.

"We would still have crashed, Alex," Drake interjected. "And it would have been worse. You would have sent us hurtling down the mountain and off a cliff."

Alex closed his eyes, memories from that dreadful night dancing across his inner vision in a macabre choreography of distorted images.

It had been the fourth of July and they'd decided to drive up to a bluff overlooking the town to watch the fireworks, all seven of them crammed in Alex's mom's dusty truck. Alex had been behind the wheel when another driver had come around a corner and jumped the center line. Alex had veered sharply to avoid his SUV and crashed into the trees lining the road.

Of the seven of them, six had walked out of Alex's mom's smashed truck with only minor cuts and bruises. Miles Martinez had not.

Although the scans Miles had over the days that followed showed no evidence of significant brain damage, he remained in a coma even after he was taken off the ventilator. As the doctor who'd been looking after the unconscious young man explained to Miles's mother, it was as if Miles had gone to sleep and decided never to wake up again.

"If you don't go in there right this minute, I'm going to put you over my shoulder and carry you to Miles's room," Drake said gruffly.

Alex's eyes snapped open at that. He frowned when he saw the teasing light in Drake's gaze. "Ha-ha, very funny."

Drake raked Alex's body with an interested stare as they climbed the steps to the porch. "You know, you've filled out pretty nicely in the last twelve years."

Alex rolled his eyes hard. "If you think that's going to make me fall in bed with you, you've got another thing coming."

Drake chuckled softly as they entered a brightly-lit reception. "Oh, I remember you 'coming' all right. You used to grip my dick so hard with your—"

Alex clamped a hand over Drake's mouth and hissed a low *"Will you shut up?!"* his ears warming while he glanced around anxiously.

Drake ran his tongue across Alex's palm.

Alex scowled and snatched his hand away.

This bastard is asking for a beating!

The woman behind the front desk watched them with a puzzled half-smile. Her expression cleared when Drake stepped out from behind Alex.

"Oh. Hi, Drake."

"Hey, Lisa."

The woman named Lisa glanced from Alex to Drake. "Who's your friend?"

"This is Alex Hancock," Drake drawled. "A former lover of mine."

Alex groaned. "Was that part strictly necessary?"

Lisa's eyes widened. She beckoned Alex closer and leaned across the counter, her expression growing conspiratorial.

"So, did he dump you or did you dump him?" she asked Alex in a low, eager voice.

"I dumped his sorry ass," Alex grumbled before Drake could say anything.

"Guilty as charged," Drake said with a dry smile. "I was an utter asshole to him."

Alex blinked at the cryptic look Drake flashed at him.

Lisa sighed and pursed her lips. "Is it wrong that I want to see the two of you in action? Like, sexually?"

Alex choked on his spit.

"Lisa's a hard core gay romance fan," Drake explained while Alex coughed and spluttered. "You'll get used to her."

"You don't say?" Alex muttered.

Lisa beamed at them without an iota of shame.

They signed the visitor's log and headed upstairs, Drake taking the lead.

A heavy feeling filled Alex's chest as they negotiated a series of corridors. He knew he was starting to panic from the way his breathing was turning shallow and fast and his pulse started to race.

Drake frowned. "Are you okay? 'Cause you look like you're about to throw up."

"I'm okay." Alex gritted his teeth. "I need to do this."

Miles's room was at the end of the building. With a dark hardwood floor and pale gray walls, it boasted dual aspect windows that commanded views of the river and the forest surrounding the facility. But it wasn't the breathtaking outlook or the pleasant decor that had Alex's heart clenching in his chest. His breath caught when his gaze landed on the sleeping man in the medical bed in the middle of the room.

Alex's vision filled with tears as he stared at Miles Martinez. He swallowed past the lump in his throat and took a step toward the bed.

"Hi, Drake," someone said quietly to his left. "Hi, Alex."

Alex turned. His heart shattered all over again.

Elaine Martinez put down her knitting and rose to her feet from the rocking chair where she'd been sitting, her movements rendered slow and awkward by her lifelong rheumatism.

Drake walked over to her and dropped a kiss on her head. "Hi, gorgeous. I swear, you look more beautiful every time I see you."

"Oh, stop that," Miles's mother murmured with a delighted chuckle, clasping his hand. Her gaze shifted to Alex, her expression growing serious.

Alex stood frozen while Elaine closed the distance between them. She gazed at him for a moment before cradling his face in her hands, her touch as gentle as he remembered it.

"You silly boy." Miles's mother wiped the tears flowing freely down Alex's cheeks with her thumbs, her own eyes glimmering with wetness. "What took you so long?"

"I'm sorry," Alex mumbled brokenly. "For everything."

Elaine shook her head. "The only thing you have to apologize for is staying away for all these years. We've missed you."

Alex closed his arms around her and buried his face in her neck, his tears soaking into her skin while his heart ached with grief. A familiar smell filled his nostrils, bringing with it a wave of fond memories. He sank into the cozy scent of cinnamon and vanilla that was Elaine Martinez, the only person in Twilight Falls who'd been able to order the "Terrible Seven" around.

It was when they were in middle school and were being threatened with expulsion after spray painting the school principal's car a racy red that Miles's mother had stepped in and unofficially adopted the gang of misfits. Not only did she spend the next seven years taking them under her wing and welcoming them into her home, she'd made sure they never strayed too far from the straight and narrow, while also allowing them the freedom to grow and make mistakes.

The hours Alex had spent in Elaine's kitchen eating the cookies she made for them while they did their homework were some of the happiest times he'd had in Twilight Falls.

Elaine had also been one of the first people Alex had come out to after his own mom and had accepted his sexuality without batting an eyelid. Although he and Drake had done their best to keep their relationship a secret, Alex suspected it hadn't escaped Elaine's notice. Not much did when it came to the seven of them.

Elaine wrapped an arm around Alex's waist and guided him to the bed. "Come say hi."

CHAPTER TWELVE

Finn's ears perked when he heard the distant sound of the front door slamming shut. He waited a moment before stepping out of the studio and making his way to the living room, trying to mask his nervousness.

Finn had spent the day being highly unproductive. In fact, if anyone were to ask him what he'd achieved since the moment Alex had walked out of the house that morning, the only reply Finn could give would be, "A giant hard-on brought on by all the fantasies I've had about Alex. Particularly Alex's lips and tongue. And his dirty, wicked mouth."

Much to his embarrassment, Finn had already jacked off several times, his body burning up and his skin prickling with awareness whenever he thought of Alex. Finn couldn't believe how thoroughly the other man had begun to fill his every waking moment or how obsessed he'd become with wanting to touch him again. To kiss him again.

Deep in Finn's mind and heart, there remained a part of him still brimming with guilt and shame. Not because of what he was feeling for Alex. But because of what he had never felt for Catherine.

Desire. Passion. Lust. The desperate need to meld his body to another in the most intimate way possible. To possess and to take.

And maybe, to be taken?

A thrill darted through Finn at that illicit notion. Of Alex claiming his body. Of Alex entering him and fucking him. Hard and fast. Slow and deep. Filling him in places he'd never been filled before. Finn's cock twitched at that sinful image. He accelerated his pace, seeking the man who was making him have such wanton thoughts.

Finn's daydreams came crashing down around him when he walked inside the living room and saw Alex.

The lawyer was standing in front of the glass wall overlooking the deck, his shoulders drooping and his palms and forehead pressed against the thick panel, as if he wanted to escape into the wilderness beyond.

Alarm flooded Finn. "Alex?"

Alex startled. A shudder raced through him. He turned.

The look on his face had Finn closing the distance between them in a few long strides. He grabbed Alex's shoulders, trepidation forming a cold pit in his stomach.

"What's wrong?!"

Alex swallowed. "I—" He faltered and took a shaky breath.

That was when Finn noticed Alex's red, swollen eyes. Something twisted inside his chest. He lifted a gentle hand to Alex's face and stroked a thumb across his flushed cheekbone. "Have you been crying?"

"Yes," Alex mumbled. "But they were good tears." He took hold of Finn's wrist. "I'm sorry. Can you—can you hold me? Just for a moment?"

Finn sensed the desperation in Alex's voice and the way his fingers clenched on his skin. He wrapped Alex into his arms wordlessly.

Alex sighed, his whole body relaxing as he leaned into Finn. He snaked his arms around Finn's waist and pressed his face against Finn's shoulder.

A serene feeling filled Finn as they stood quietly bathed in the late afternoon light. He could feel the steady, strong thump of Alex's heart beating against his own. Finn closed his eyes and buried his face in Alex's hair.

It had been a long time since he'd experienced such peacefulness. And he owed it all to the man he was holding. The man who'd stormed into his life and was awakening his dormant heart. The desire he'd been suppressing for the last few days surged through him once more.

Alex stiffened slightly in his arms a moment later. "Finn?"

"Yeah?"

"Why are you hard?"

Finn started to pull away, mortified at his body's unconscious reaction. Alex tightened his hold around

Finn's waist and raised his head. Finn met his curious stare, his own cheeks flaming with embarrassment.

"What are you thinking about right now?" Alex murmured.

Finn hesitated. "That I'm a bastard."

Alex's lips lifted in a smile. "Wrong answer."

Finn's breath caught. That was all it took to light up Alex's face. A simple, sweet smile.

"I'm recalling all the filthy thoughts I've had about you since you left the house this morning," he admitted huskily.

Alex's pupils flared at Finn's confession. "And exactly what kind of filthy thoughts have you been having about me, Mr. West?"

Finn's heart pounded in time with his throbbing erection when he noted the slight catch in Alex's voice and the faint flush of color on the lawyer's cheekbones. He took one of Alex's hands and lowered it boldly to his groin.

Alex stilled when his fingers made contact with the rigid flesh tenting the front of Finn's jeans.

"I've been thinking about how I want you to do something about *this*," Finn said in a low voice. "I've jerked off three times today. And I'm still hard."

He swallowed a curse when Alex gently stroked his shaft, shocked at the sudden bolt of pleasure the action brought him.

"Does that feel good?" Alex breathed.

"*Yes!*" Finn hissed.

Alex's eyes grew feverish as he started working

Finn's erection in earnest, the pain that had clouded his face replaced by desire.

Finn surrendered to his instincts, curled his fingers in Alex's hair, and lowered his head to take Alex's mouth.

Alex arched into Finn as Finn initiated a slow, deep kiss. He hooked one hand behind Finn's neck and kept his other hand busy on Finn's dick while Finn mated their tongues together.

The emotions bubbling under Finn's skin exploded into full blown hunger as he tasted Alex and explored the hot depths of his mouth.

The man was simply addictive.

The sound of a belt being unbuckled and a zipper being opened reached Finn dimly. He gasped when Alex slipped a hand inside his briefs and cupped his erection.

"Fuck," Finn mumbled against Alex's mouth.

Rationality fled Finn's mind when Alex started rubbing his shaft. He had never known such wicked pleasure before.

I need to see!

Alex opened his eyes when Finn reluctantly broke their kiss. Finn's dick throbbed painfully at the passionate light darkening the blue gaze beneath him. He looked down and froze.

The sight of Alex's fingers on his naked cock was the most breathtakingly sinful thing Finn had ever seen. Alex panted and bucked his hips while he continued stroking Finn, his touch growing urgent and slick with Finn's precum.

That was when Finn realized just how hard Alex was.

The repulsion he thought he would experience at sensing another man's erection against his own body never manifested itself. Instead, all he could think about was how sexy Alex looked right now.

Finn crowded Alex against the glass wall and dropped his hands to Alex's belt, eager to make Alex experience the same ecstasy he was so generously giving him. Alex stiffened when Finn hurriedly unbuckled his pants and drew his zipper down.

"Finn? Are you—" Alex stopped and let out the most erotic sound Finn had ever heard when Finn slid a hand inside his briefs and freed his rock hard dick.

"*Oh God!*" Alex gasped, fingers biting into Finn's nape.

Finn's blood roared in his ears as he started exploring Alex's stiff length. He stroked the pulsing veins and marveled at the glistening, flushed skin covering Alex's cock, enthralled by how aroused touching Alex's erection was making him feel.

In that moment, Finn wanted nothing more than to see Alex explode under him.

Alex's breath hitched in his throat as Finn rubbed the pad of his thumb across the wet tip of his dick. Finn grunted when Alex's fingers clenched reflexively on his own throbbing organ. He braced one hand on the glass wall next to Alex's head and pressed his body against Alex's.

Their fingers touched where they were desperately stroking each other.

Finn grabbed Alex's hand and gently tugged him off his own cock.

"What—" Alex mumbled, confused.

"Together," Finn whispered against his mouth.

Alex's eyes widened as Finn guided him to take both their shafts in his grip, just as he did too. Finn hissed at the sensation of Alex's hot, hard cock straining against his own rigid flesh. He kissed Alex and swept his tongue inside the other man's mouth once more.

Alex trembled, his dick twitching uncontrollably in Finn's grasp. He groaned and dropped his head back, breaking their kiss.

A fiery feeling of possession washed over Finn at the sight of Alex's flushed cheeks and the sound of his ragged breathing.

He could tell just how much pleasure Alex was getting from his touch. That he, Finn West, was making this sexy, confident man shiver and shudder in his arms excited him like little else could.

Finn lowered his head and pressed his mouth to Alex's throat. He kissed the hot skin covering Alex's throbbing pulse and felt a savage thrill when Alex bucked in his hold.

"*Finn!*"

Delicious tension wound through Finn's lower body. He accelerated the pace of his hand as the sensation arrowed in on his cock and balls.

"*Yes!*" Alex moaned. "Faster!"

Finn groaned when Alex tightened his grip on their flesh.

"Harder, Alex!" he growled against Alex's throat before nipping his skin with his teeth.

The soft bite was all it took for Alex to come. He cried out and rose on his tip toes, his body convulsing against Finn, his hot cum splashing over their hands and Finn's T-shirt.

Pressure built in Finn's lower belly. He gasped when the first ripple of an intense orgasm exploded inside his body. Finn squeezed his eyes shut and let out a hoarse shout against Alex's throat. Blood roared in his skull as violent waves of pleasure sent his cock throbbing and pulsing out cum in Alex's hand. He rolled and thrust his groin against Alex's, meeting Alex's wildly pumping hips.

It was a while before Finn became aware of his surroundings. He was leaning into Alex where they stood against the glass wall, his face buried in the crook of Alex's neck. Alex's pulse thumped rapidly under Finn's cheek, his chest rising and falling raggedly against Finn's frame.

Finn took a shuddering breath and slowly raised his head.

The sight that met his eyes almost made him hard again.

Alex was looking at him dazedly, his eyes indigo with pleasure. Color stained his cheekbones a lovely shade of pink and his blond hair was all mussed up from Finn's touch.

Finn had never seen anyone as beautiful as Alex in the wake of his climax.

A sated smile curved Alex's lips. He looked down at

their cum-filled hands. "Was this what you were thinking about the whole day?"

Finn let out a satisfied sigh and pressed his forehead against Alex's. "Among other things."

Alex chuckled.

"I WANT YOU TO MODEL FOR ME," FINN SAID.

Alex stared at Finn.

It was morning and they were lying in bed, their breathing still fast and ragged from the orgasm they'd just given each other. Alex was surprised they'd managed to sleep much the last few nights, considering how hot and hard and hungry Finn had been since their first handjob. It was as if he were making up for all the years he'd never experienced these feelings.

Although Alex had sensed Finn wanted to do more, he'd held back from making any advances beyond kissing and touching Finn. This had as much to do with the inexplicable guilt he was suddenly experiencing over Finn's dead wife, as it did with his bruised heart following his trip to the long-term care facility yesterday.

Alex had finally spoken to Finn about Miles and the accident two nights ago. Finn had listened wordlessly before taking Alex in his arms and quietly telling him what everyone else had been saying to Alex for the last twelve years. That it hadn't been his fault.

Although he had known Finn only for a little while, Alex couldn't help the intense relief he'd felt at Finn's comforting words. Still, he didn't think he could swallow Finn's rejection if he were to suggest they moved beyond handjobs.

Alex had decided to wait for Finn to make the next move. And something told him it wouldn't be too long before that happened.

"Model?" Alex repeated. He grimaced. "As in, what? Nude modeling?"

Finn chuckled. "Not quite. I have an idea for a sculpture for my art exhibition." He paused, his expression turning serious. "It's going to be the central piece. And I need a model for it."

Alex's ears warmed under Finn's stare. He couldn't believe Finn wanted to feature him in his art exhibition. He wondered whether the artist realized just how big a deal that was.

"Why me?"

Finn pushed himself up on an elbow and reached across the space separating them to stroke a gentle hand across Alex's cheek.

"Because this piece is about passion. And right now, the one I'm passionate about is you."

Heat flooded Alex's face. "Just so you know, if it were anyone else but you saying that, it would come off as seriously corny."

Finn arched an eyebrow. "But?"

Alex turned his face and pressed a warm kiss

against Finn's knuckles. "From you, it's a goddamn miracle. And I'm glad I'm the reason behind it."

Finn's eyes darkened. He curled a hand at the back of Alex's head and leaned in to take his mouth in a fierce kiss. Alex parted his lips and welcomed Finn inside, his dick twitching with fresh arousal.

Finn shuffled over and shifted his larger frame over Alex's. Alex couldn't help but groan at the heady feeling of Finn's weight pressing him into the mattress and the hard angles of the body molded intimately to his. Finn broke their kiss, nudged Alex's chin up, and pressed his lips to Alex's throat.

"Finn?" Alex murmured dazedly, shivers jolting him as Finn nipped and sucked his heated flesh.

"Yeah?"

"I'm seeing a client at ten."

Finn grew still. "Damn." He raised his head and studied the clock on his nightstand with a focused frown. "That's twenty minutes to ride into town, fifteen for breakfast, and ten for you get dressed," he mumbled. His expression brightened. "That means we have just under twelve minutes."

He lifted off Alex, grabbed Alex's hand, and tugged him off the bed.

Alex blinked, confused, as Finn led him in the direction of the bathroom.

"For what?"

Finn flashed him a scorching look over his shoulder. "For me to find out exactly how enticing your dick looks all hard and wet and covered with soap suds."

Alex groaned, his cock hardening at Finn's filthy words. "I've awakened a beast."

Finn grinned. "The beast says thanks. Now, let's get you out of those pajamas."

ജ

"You look like the cat that got the cream."

Alex startled and looked at Hunter where he sat opposite him.

It was mid-afternoon and they were having coffee around the corner from Hunter's shop and Alex's new office.

"Do I?" Alex murmured, trying hard to suppress the smile he'd worn most of that morning.

Much to his chagrin, Alex had spent his time between his client appointments thinking about the things he and Finn had done to each other in the shower several hours ago. All the hot, wet, wicked things.

To Finn's delight, they'd discovered that the bathroom had great acoustics. Alex's cheeks warmed.

Thank God we don't have neighbors. I don't think I've ever moaned that loud in my life!

Hunter narrowed his eyes. "Yeah, you do. You also look like someone who's been thoroughly fucked."

Alex hushed him and glanced around the coffee shop.

The women at the next table turned and stared at them.

"Will you keep it down?" Alex hissed at Hunter.

Hunter flashed an apologetic smile at the woman before leaning closer to Alex. "Spill it, Hancock."

Alex bit his lip as the torrid image of him coming all over Finn's greedy hands a few hours ago flashed across his inner vision.

Yeah, I spilled a lot. So did he.

"I don't know what you're talking about."

Hunter snorted. "So, you're telling me you and the artist aren't—" he lowered his voice, "doing the dance of the two-headed beast?"

"If you mean sex, then the answer is no," Alex said tartly.

"Aha!" Hunter pulled back and pointed an accusing finger at Alex. "So, you're not denying you've done other stuff."

Alex rolled his eyes. "No, Your Honor. I'm not denying anything."

Hunter grinned. "You guys been—" He looked around to make sure no one was looking their way, turned sideways in his chair, and made a not-so-subtle jerking off motion with his hand.

Alex sighed. "You're despicable, you know that?"

"Ah, come on," Hunter ribbed. "I'm a gay guy in a town with very few hot gay men. Indulge me."

Alex muttered something rude under his breath.

The bell above the front door jangled. He bit back a curse when he looked over Hunter's shoulder and saw the two men who'd just walked inside the coffee shop.

"Hey," Tristan called out. He made his way toward their table, Drake following in his wake. "What are you guys up to?"

"Having coffee," Alex said sullenly.

"Talking about Alex's sex life," Hunter gushed with a grin.

Drake glanced at Alex's wedding ring as he took the seat next to Hunter. Alex tried not to squirm under his potent stare.

Although he suspected Drake had wanted to question him about it when they'd met at the care facility, it was Elaine who'd asked Alex about the ring. The shocked expression on her face when Alex had explained the circumstances behind his marriage to Finn had been reflected in the depths of Drake's hard eyes. The same hard eyes he was looking at Alex with right now.

Tristan's gaze switched from Alex to Drake and back again, clearly picking up on the tense vibe between the two of them.

"You and the artist are making out?" Tristan asked lightly.

Alex narrowed his eyes. "That's none of your business."

"I thought sex wasn't part of this fake marriage agreement of yours," Drake said.

Alex frowned at Drake's emphasis on the word *fake.* "It isn't."

"So, what then? You like this guy?" Drake challenged.

Alex was conscious of Tristan's guarded stare and Hunter's puzzled one. He'd always wondered if anyone else in their group bar Izzy had known about his and Drake's relationship before he'd left Twilight Falls.

From the expression on Tristan's face, at least one of them had.

Alex met Drake's irate gaze head on. "I do, actually. More than I'd care to admit."

Hunter and Tristan arched their eyebrows at Alex's blunt statement. A muscle jumped in Drake's jawline. Alex clenched his teeth.

What's his problem?

"So, you guys heard the latest on Carter?" Hunter said in a falsely bright voice.

"No," Alex muttered, grateful for Hunter's obvious attempt to defuse the strained atmosphere. "What's he done now?"

"Not what. It's more like *who* has he done. As in multiple."

CHAPTER FOURTEEN

Finn studied Alex with a faint frown where the latter sat toying with his salad opposite him. "Are you okay?"

Alex startled and looked up. "Hmm. Yeah, I'm fine."

"You don't look fine," Finn said, unconvinced.

"I'm sorry. It's just—" Alex faltered and rubbed the back of his head, his lips twisting in a grimace. "I've got something on my mind is all."

"Is it what we did this morning?"

Alex looked at him blankly. Color stained his cheeks when he realized what Finn meant. "No! God, *that* had me hot and horny most of the day. It's a miracle my clients didn't notice."

Relief flooded Finn. He wasn't going to admit to Alex that he'd spent his day in a similar state. Or that he was dying to repeat their wicked shower sex session all over again. Finn had been right about one thing.

Alex's cock had looked particularly delicious covered in soap suds.

"Is it the modeling?" Finn said.

Alex shook his head. "No, it isn't that either."

Finn bit back a sigh. It was obvious the lawyer wasn't ready to talk about what was bothering him yet. That fact made Finn feel surprisingly frustrated.

"Good," he murmured. "Because I was thinking we could start tonight, if you're up to it."

Surprise widened Alex's eyes. "Oh. Hmm, okay."

They cleared the table and headed to Finn's studio. Finn could literally see Alex tensing up as he switched the lights on and motioned him to the modelling stool in the middle of the room. Alex perched on the seat and followed Finn with his eyes while he moved around the studio.

Finn positioned his drawing easel and chair at a slight angle from where Alex sat. He looked up and sighed at the nervous expression pasted across Alex's face.

"Relax, Alex. I'm only going to draw you."

Alex bit his lip. "Sorry. I've never done this before. You'll have to tell me what you want me to do."

Finn nodded. "Can you take your T-shirt and shoes off?"

Alex hesitated before murmuring a low, "Sure." He reached for the hem of his top, stripped it off over his head, and kicked his loafers to the floor.

Finn took the T-shirt from Alex's white-knuckled grip and laid it on one of the worktops. He paused, his back to Alex.

"You know, we don't have to do this right now if you don't want to. Or ever."

Taut silence filled the studio.

"I want to," Alex finally said. "To be honest, I could do with the distraction."

Finn turned and dipped his chin, doing his best to hide his relief. Now that he'd resolved to use Alex as his model, all he could think about was the piece he wanted to make. It had been a long time since he'd felt this excited about a new project.

"Is there anything else you need me to do?" Alex murmured.

Though Alex probably meant nothing by it, his question brought a sudden, hot memory flashing across Finn's inner vision. Finn clenched his teeth.

Now's really not the time to be getting horny, West.

"Just sit as naturally as you can."

"Okay."

Ten minutes later, Finn put his charcoal stick down.

Alex stiffened. "What?"

"Your pose isn't quite right."

Alex blinked. "Oh."

Finn rose and headed over to the modelling stool.

"Bend your knee like this." He took hold of Alex's right leg and moved his foot to the foot rest. "And angle your face like so."

A hint of color suffused Alex's cheeks when Finn clasped his chin and turned his head slightly.

"Is that better?" Alex mumbled.

Finn bit back a smile at the throaty catch in Alex's voice.

So, I'm not the only one who's turned on.

"One more thing." He moved his hands to Alex's

chest and deliberately ran his fingers over his skin before adjusting the angle of his shoulders.

Alex jumped slightly at the contact. Finn's cock stirred when he saw Alex's nipples harden. He forced himself to go back to his seat and pick up the charcoal stick.

Sexual awareness prickled Finn's skin as the minutes ticked by. The same awareness that was raising goosebumps on Alex's skin and making his breathing speed up and his face flush.

Alex shifted slightly on the stool.

Finn's gaze dropped to Alex's groin. He nearly groaned out loud when he saw the splendid erection Alex was desperately trying to hide.

"You're hard," Finn said, his tone almost accusing.

Alex grimaced. "Sorry. It's just—well, it's because you're looking at me like—" He stopped and waved a hand vaguely.

"Like what?" Finn said, intrigued.

"Like you want to eat me up," Alex blurted out. "I mean, I'd have to be a freaking saint not to get turned on when you're staring at me like you want to swallow me whole."

Finn blinked. He hadn't realized he'd been watching Alex with such open yearning.

He's right. I do want to eat him up. All the way from his mussed up hair to his delectable toes.

Finn put the charcoal stick down. There was no point pretending like he was going to be able to draw much of anything tonight.

"Would you like that?"

Alex stared. "Like what?"

A naughty impulse blasted through Finn. He rose, walked over to a countertop, and picked up a large, round painting brush from a pot. Alex's pupils dilated as Finn closed the distance to the modelling stool.

"For me to eat you up." Finn stopped in front of Alex. "Like here, for example."

Alex shivered when Finn ran the brush lightly over his throat. His breath caught as Finn worked the bristles teasingly across his left collarbone.

"And here," Finn said huskily.

Alex gasped when Finn lowered the brush and traced his right nipple, his heated expression telling Finn exactly what he thought about the provocative sex play Finn had just initiated.

"What about here?" Finn moved his knuckles to Alex's straining cock. "Would you like me to eat you here too, Alex?"

Alex grasped the edges of the stool, body arching instinctively into Finn's touch as Finn stroked him lightly. "Shit. That feels good!"

Finn's dick throbbed. It wasn't the answer he'd been looking for but he'd take it. He placed the brush on a table, reached for Alex's shoulders, and leaned down.

Alex tensed when Finn's breath washed across his left nipple. Finn paused.

"Finn?" Alex breathed.

"Yes, Alex?" Finn's erection pressed painfully against the zipper of his jeans as he waited, his mouth hovering above Alex's nipple.

Alex clutched Finn's head with one hand and tugged him closer.

Finn opened his lips and gave Alex what he was so clearly begging for. Alex let out a low moan as Finn closed his lips on his left nipple. He shuddered and jerked in Finn's grasp when Finn circled and flicked the hot, hard nub teasingly with his tongue before sucking it into the velvety depths of his mouth.

"Oh!"

Frenzied desire exploded inside Finn at Alex's throaty cry. He straightened and took Alex's mouth in a hungry kiss before moving his mouth back to Alex's throat and chest, eager to explore Alex's body with his lips and tongue. He feasted hungrily on the pulse thrumming at the base of Alex's throat and his sensitive nipples before moving to his pecs and ribs.

Alex's breathing grew labored as Finn trailed his softly-defined six-pack with his mouth and pressed his lips to his quivering belly. Finn unfastened the button at the top of Alex's jeans and pulled Alex's zipper down.

They both groaned when Alex's cock sprung free in Finn's hands. Alex gripped Finn's shoulders, his touch desperate.

"You're driving me crazy!"

Finn looked up into Alex's frantic eyes and did what he'd wanted to do. Been *dying* to do for days. He went down on his knees, spread Alex's legs open, and kissed a torrid path from Alex's navel all the way down the strip of dark blond hair arrowing towards Alex's dick.

"Finn!"

Alex's hoarse shout echoed against the glass walls as Finn slowly and deliberately licked his cock from the root all the way to the trembling, engorged, wet tip. The scent of Alex's precum struck Finn's nostrils. His own dick jerked at the musky, earthy smell.

He laved and kissed Alex's shaft, his ravenous tongue and lips bumping across the ridges of veins covering Alex's turgid flesh, the thatch of hair crowning the base of Alex's sex tickling his nose.

Finn growled. Alex tasted like sweet sin. And Finn wanted more of the luscious flavor. He tightened his grip on Alex's thighs, moved his lips to the head of Alex's cock, and took him inside his mouth.

He might as well have set off a bomb from the way Alex stiffened and cried out above him.

Finn breathed through his nose as he explored the rigid cock filling his cheeks and throbbing against his lips. He wasn't going to admit to Alex that he'd been reading up on blowjobs and gay sex. Or that he'd watched porn videos he'd found on an adult site online and had jacked off more times than he'd care to admit while he'd pictured Alex and him in place of the actors on the screen.

"*Oh, Jesus!*" Alex gasped as Finn rolled his tongue around his shaft. "Where did you learn how to do that?!"

Finn raised his eyes and met Alex's stunned stare. He smiled around Alex's cock, hollowed his cheeks, and sucked. Alex cried out and clutched the back of Finn's head, his hips thrusting his dick deeper into Finn's mouth.

Finn braced Alex's thighs open with his shoulders, moved his hands to Alex's butt, and took a firm hold of his toned flesh. He drew his lips and tongue up Alex's shaft to the broad, hot head of his cock, licked the precum oozing out of the tip, and bobbed down again, taking Alex all the way to the back of his throat.

An incoherent sound left Alex as Finn started blowing him in earnest. He gasped and moaned and keened, his hips rolling deeply as he surrendered to his desire and fucked Finn's mouth, his body twitching and trembling uncontrollably with pleasure.

Finn kept his gaze locked on Alex's as he pulled Alex's jeans down his hips.

Alex's eyes widened when Finn spread his butt cheeks and ran a finger down his crack. They fluttered closed when Finn found the soft pucker of his hole.

Lust slammed into Finn as he explored the tight folds of skin covering Alex's entrance. Never in a thousand years could he have imagined that he would be on his knees in his studio one day, blowing a man toward an orgasm while he played with his ass. Or that he would be reveling in it so much.

The sounds Alex made. The taste of his cock and precum on Finn's tongue. The heat of his rock-hard flesh hitting the back of Finn's throat with hungry hard thrusts. The feel of his back passage spasming against the pad of Finn's finger.

Finn loved it all.

Alex suddenly went rigid above Finn. He grasped Finn's hair and tried to tug him off his dick. "Finn, stop! I'm gonna—"

Finn pushed his finger inside Alex's ass and sucked hard, his hungry gaze on Alex's face.

Alex came violently, his entire body tightening like a bow, his mouth open on harsh grunts, his face and chest red from the force of his climax. Hot cum exploded inside Finn's mouth as he thrust his finger repeatedly inside Alex's ass, mimicking Alex's pumping hips. He swallowed the sticky, musky evidence of Alex's orgasm before licking and tenderly kissing the cock pulsating against his cheeks.

Sweat dripped off Alex's nose as he shuddered and panted above Finn. Finn slipped his finger out of Alex's back passage and let go of Alex's dripping cock.

"Was that good?" he asked huskily, his cheeks and ears warming as the realization of the line they'd just crossed.

The fire in Alex's eyes was all the answer Finn needed.

"I really want to know where you learned to do that," Alex groaned. "But I gotta do something else first."

Finn chuckled when Alex climbed off the stool, yanked him to his feet, and tugged him across the studio. His amusement faded as Alex pushed his back against the glass wall and went down on his knees in front of him.

Finn's breath hitched in his throat when Alex gripped his zipper with his teeth and tugged it down tantalizing over his aching erection, his hot blue gaze locked unblinkingly on Finn's.

Alex yanked Finn's jeans down to his knees and

took Finn's cock inside his mouth in a single hungry gulp.

Finn hissed and dropped his head against the cool glass, fingers spearing Alex's hair with desperate urgency, eager to experience what he'd just done to Alex. He groaned as Alex's clever lips, tongue, and fingers started working his shaft like a virtuoso, no longer shocked at the sinful pleasure only Alex could give him.

It didn't take long for Finn to explode at the back of Alex's throat. And he did so with gusto, his hips pumping Alex's mouth furiously while he fixed Alex's head in a punishing grip, his hoarse shouts of ecstasy echoing around his studio for what felt like endless moments.

CHAPTER FIFTEEN

Izzy narrowed her eyes at Finn where she perched on a stool at the kitchen island. "What's wrong with you?"

"Nothing's wrong with me." Finn finished pouring their coffee and brought the cups across to where she sat.

"That sappy smile isn't nothing."

Finn blinked. "Was I smiling?"

"Yeah, you were. And like I said, it was sappy."

Finn bit the inside of his cheek to stop himself from grinning. He couldn't stop smiling. And it had everything to do with a certain blue-eyed blond who'd been filling his dreams lately.

Just like I filled his mouth again this morning.

Finn's ears grew hot. He and Alex had gone on to blow each other several times over after the episode in the studio three nights ago. Their latest session in the shower an hour ago had been particularly loud and torrid.

There was one more startling thing Finn had realized that morning. He was sleeping again. Properly sleeping. Despite the fact that he and Alex had been all over each other lately, Finn felt more rested than he'd been in years.

The object of his fantasies waltzed into the kitchen.

"Hey, Izzy." Alex dropped a kiss on the brunette's head and went to pour himself a coffee.

"Hi, Alex," Izzy murmured. Her eyes narrowed again a moment later. "Gawd, you're doing it too."

Alex looked over at her. "Doing what?"

"Smiling sappily," Izzy snapped. "If I didn't know any better, I'd say you two were—" She stopped and sucked in air. Her eyes rounded to the size of saucers at the same time she clutched her face with her hands. *"Oh my God, you two are fucking, aren't you?!"*

Alex stiffened and exchanged a startled glance with Finn.

Guilt pierced Finn when he saw the anxious expression darkening Alex's eyes. He'd suspected the lawyer had been worried about what Finn would think if someone were to find out about them. Finn hadn't been too sure himself how he would feel if and when that situation arose.

Now that it had, he had his answer.

"Busted," Finn said with a slow grin. He crossed the floor and pressed his lips to Alex's. "Look at it this way. Now I can manhandle you in front of her."

Izzy let out a delighted squeal.

Alex froze before relaxing, relief washing across his

face. He searched Finn's eyes nervously. "You don't mind?"

"If other people know?" Finn arched an eyebrow. "I'd put out a PSA if you'd let me."

A bark of laughter escaped Alex then. He snaked his hands around Finn's waist and dropped his face against Finn's shoulder, chuckles shaking him. Finn hugged Alex, amazed at how natural it felt to be holding the man in his arms.

They became aware of a heated stare.

"I want to know every filthy, sticky detail," Izzy stated, a zealous light brightening her green eyes. "Particularly the sticky bit."

Finn and Alex groaned out loud at the same time.

"It shouldn't be difficult to get a restraining order against your husband," Alex told the distressed woman in front of him. "There's enough evidence from the police reports and the hospital for me to make the case to the judge."

His client hesitated, her eyes wide with fear.

"It's alright, Casey," the woman next to her said with a determined expression. "This has gone on for far too long. He broke your arm. Next time, it might be your skull."

"Your friend is right, Casey," Alex said gently.

His client took a shaky breath and dipped her chin.

"Have you got somewhere to stay?" Alex said. "It's not safe for you to go back to the house."

Casey's friend raised her chin. "She's staying with me."

Alex smiled, relieved. "Good."

The pair left his office a short while later.

Alex sat back in his chair and looked out of the window. A light shower was falling across Twilight Falls, bringing forth the vivid greens and reds of the valley.

His new business was doing better than he'd ever dreamed it would. Alex wasn't sure if it was his reputation as a former city lawyer or the fact that he'd grown up in Twilight Falls that meant he now had appointments lined up for the next three weeks.

He'd just finished filling in the petition for the restraining order against Casey's husband when his cell phone rang. Alex tensed when he saw the number on the screen. He took the call, his heart thumping and his fingers trembling slightly.

"Hello?"

A crisp, female voice rose at the other end of the line.

"Mr. Hancock? This is FBI agent Barnes. We've got a lead on Ryan Fisher. He was spotted in Monterrey two days ago, about a hundred miles south of Texas border. We think he might be trying to get back in the country."

Alex's hand tightened on his phone. This was the phone call he'd long been waiting for and never thought he would receive.

"He has a cousin in Austin," he said stiffly. "That might be where he's headed."

"We suspected as much. We've had people watching his cousin's house since yesterday. I'll let you know when we have further news. And ring me if he contacts you."

"I will," Alex mumbled. "Thank you."

He was still staring at his cell when his office door opened and Hunter wandered in.

"Hey, aren't we supposed to be catching lunch?"

"Sorry," Alex mumbled distractedly, still shaken by the unexpected conversation. "I just got an important call."

Hunter's expression grew serious. "You okay?"

Alex nodded. He told Hunter about the FBI closing in on his former business partner.

Hunter's face brightened up. "That's great! Does that mean you might see some of the money he stole from you?"

Alex grimaced. "I doubt that. Knowing Ryan, he's probably gambled away most of it."

Hunter leaned a hip against Alex's desk. "Well, I've got some news that might cheer you up. I'm having a barbecue this Saturday."

"A barbecue?" Alex raised his eyebrows. "Isn't it a bit early for that?"

"Not according to the weatherman. It's gonna be scorching hot this weekend, so I thought I'd have everyone over and break in my new grill. You can bring Finn too, if he wants to come."

Suspicion bloomed inside Alex. "Wait. This isn't a ploy for you guys to meet Finn, is it?"

Hunter pressed a hand to his chest in a gesture of

innocence. "I am hurt that you would even suggest that."

Alex scowled. "I'm right though, aren't I?"

Hunter grinned. "If he's gonna be part of your life, then don't you think it's a good idea for us to get to know him?"

Hunter's words made Alex's heart stutter and brought the cold reality of his and Finn's situation to the forefront of his mind once more.

However much he and Finn were enjoying their time together, there was no denying that their relationship was based on a fake marriage and that their agreement would end in five months.

Will Finn still be part of my life after that?

"So, how about it?" Hunter said, oblivious to Alex's troubled thoughts.

Hunter's cell dinged, buying Alex a moment of grace. He took his phone out of the back pocket of his jeans and glanced at the message lighting up his screen. His eyes widened. He looked up jerkily at Alex.

"Wait. You're sleeping with Finn?!"

"What the—" Alex jumped to his feet, stormed around his desk, and grabbed Hunter's phone off him. He swore when he saw Izzy's message. "You guys have a group chat?!"

"Well, yeah." Hunter stared at Alex. "So, you two are fuck buddies, huh?"

"Don't put it so crudely," Alex snapped.

Hunter's eyes grew thoughtful. "Are you saying it's more than that?"

Alex opened and closed his mouth soundlessly, the unexpected question echoing in his ears.

Is it? More than just great sex? Am I—am I falling for Finn?

Hunter's question still weighed heavily on Alex's mind when he rode home that night. And it resonated inside him long after he and Finn had given each other blowjobs and handjobs, their passion undiminished.

It was as moonlight peeked from between the clouds hanging over the forest and washed across their bed, illuminating Finn's face where he slept beside Alex, that Alex finally admitted the truth he'd been denying this whole time.

He was losing his heart to Finn West.

CHAPTER SIXTEEN

Finn stepped out of his Jeep, his palms sweaty with nerves. Alex came around the vehicle and took his hand. The lawyer squinted at him.

"Are you okay? You look like you're gonna throw up."

"I'm fine," Finn muttered.

He stared from the other vehicles parked on the driveway around them to the sprawling log and brick lodge backing onto private woodland.

Hunter Thomson's home was at the end of a gated estate on the edge of Twilight Falls. From the look of the property and its location, the guy was doing pretty well for himself.

When Alex had asked Finn if he'd like to come to his friend's place for a barbecue that weekend, Finn had found himself more than a little intrigued. He didn't know much about Alex's friends bar the titbits he'd heard from Izzy over the time he'd known her, and he realized that he wanted to rectify that situation.

Now that he was actually here though, Finn felt more anxious than he thought he would be. In fact, he hadn't felt this apprehensive about something in a long time.

Shit. It's almost like we're dating and I'm about to meet his family.

"Relax, they're not gonna eat you." Alex tugged on Finn's hand and led him up the gravel path to the lodge.

The front door opened as they climbed the steps to the wide, wrap around porch. A man with a shock of wavy, dark hair and slate gray eyes appeared in the doorway, a beer in hand.

"Hi, Alex," the stranger said with a warm smile. His expression sobered as he looked at Finn. He leaned against the doorjamb and levelled a serious stare at the artist. "You must be Finn. Before I allow you into my home, I must ask you an important question."

Alex frowned.

"Yes?" Finn said hesitantly.

"What are your intentions toward Alex?"

Alex's jaw dropped open. "Sweet Jesus, Hunter!" he spluttered once he could speak again. "Who are you, my mother?!"

Hunter sniffed. "Well, I see myself more as your father, actually."

"I'm two months older than you," Alex said between gritted teeth.

"Hey!" Izzy shouted from inside the house. "Ask them who's topping whom!"

"*Izzy!*" a pair of male voices groaned simultaneously while a third one snorted.

"What?" Izzy said defensively.

Finn started to laugh, the tension that had plagued him on the drive over vanishing like mist in the sun. The sound startled Alex and Hunter.

"I'm sorry," Finn managed between chuckles, "but has Izzy always been so—"

"Shy?" Hunter's mouth split in a warm grin. "She's a regular wall flower. Come on in before she starts grilling you two about your sex life in front of the neighbors."

Finn and Alex followed Hunter through a charming living room with a fireplace and down a hallway to a kitchen at the back of the house. Izzy stood leaning against a counter on the left, next to a man Finn recognized as Izzy's older brother.

"Wyatt," Alex greeted with a grimace.

"Hey, Alex." Wyatt Batista smiled at Finn, his green eyes curious. "It's good to see you again, Finn."

Izzy sneaked a hand in the salad Wyatt was busy making and nabbed an olive.

Wyatt frowned at her. "That's the tenth one you've stolen in the last five minutes."

Izzy wrinkled her nose at her older brother. "But you still love me, right?"

Wyatt let out a long suffering sigh that drew a chuckle from one of the other two figures in the kitchen. Finn turned toward them, curious.

"Hi, I'm Tristan," said the man with the serious

brown eyes who was marinating some chicken. "Tristan Hart."

Finn dipped his chin. "Finn West."

"And I'm Nathan, a friend of Wyatt's," the man who'd laughed said with a smile, his blue eyes twinkling with amusement. He took a swig of his beer and glanced from Finn to Alex. "So, who *is* topping whom?"

Alex groaned.

Izzy grinned. "I like this guy," she told Wyatt, jabbing an olive at Nathan.

Finn and Alex accepted the beers Hunter handed them and followed the group into the backyard a short while later. It was clear to Finn from Alex's interactions with his friends that he cared for them deeply. And Finn could see why.

Despite the fact that he was a stranger to most of them, the men Alex had grown up with were treating Finn as if he were one of their own.

Finn helped them set the table while Hunter fired up the barbecue. He'd just finished his beer when the rumble of a powerful engine rose from the front of the house. Alex stiffened where he stood next to Finn. Finn glanced at him curiously.

The front door slammed in the distance. A tall man with dark blue eyes and brown hair that teased the collar of his jacket appeared at the back door a moment later, a couple of six-packs in hand.

"Hey, Drake," Hunter called out. "I'm glad you could make it."

"Wouldn't miss it for the world." The stranger's gaze

landed on Alex briefly before shifting to Finn. "You must be Finn." He stepped down into the yard, put the cans on the table, and came over to shake Finn's hand. "I'm Drake Jackson."

"Finn West," Finn murmured. Surprise jolted him when he registered Drake's callused grip. "You work with your hands?"

Drake smiled faintly. "I'm a builder."

"Drake made this lodge for me," Hunter said with a proud grin.

Finn studied the handsome lines of Hunter's home with fresh eyes. "I like your work."

"Thanks." Drake glanced at Alex. "I hear you've got quite a nice place yourself up in the forest."

"You guys should come over one day," Finn said lightly.

As the long, lazy afternoon wore on, Finn couldn't help but note the mild strain in Alex's composure whenever he spoke to Drake. Though he wanted to ask Alex why he seemed so tense around the man, Finn knew he didn't have the right to question the lawyer about his friends. He'd just gone inside the lodge to use the restroom when he bumped into Tristan in the kitchen.

"Need a hand with that?" Finn indicated the bottles of soda and water Tristan had taken out of the fridge.

"Sure."

They were about to step out the back door when Tristan placed a hand on Finn's arm and halted him in his tracks.

"About Drake and Alex," Tristan murmured. He

looked to where Alex sat talking to Nathan, Wyatt, and Izzy at the table. "Don't pay any attention to them. Drake is just being a grouch. And Alex's gone on the defensive."

Finn followed Tristan's gaze to where Drake was helping Hunter at the grill. "Is there some bad blood between them?"

A laconic smile twisted Tristan's lips. "Not really. Let's just say they used to be real close in the past and leave it at that."

Finn headed after Tristan, puzzled by the other man's cryptic words.

Alex looked at him curiously when he sat next to him. "What's wrong?"

Finn realized he was frowning. He relaxed and smiled at Alex. "It's nothing."

Something made Finn look around. He stiffened when he saw Drake staring at Alex. The builder met Finn's eyes boldly before answering whatever question Hunter had just asked him.

That was when the truth smacked Finn in the face.

Drake and Alex used to be lovers.

CHAPTER SEVENTEEN

ALEX STUDIED FINN THOUGHTFULLY AS THE LATTER negotiated the steep mountain road, the Jeep's headlights cutting crisply through the darkness ahead.

"You've been pretty quiet since we left Hunter's place. Are you sure you're okay?"

"I'm fine," Finn murmured.

Alex narrowed his eyes. He could tell Finn was lying.

"You don't look fine." A sudden thought occurred to Alex. He made a face. "Did you not like my friends?"

This time, Finn's expression cleared. "I did, actually. Like them, I mean." He glanced at Alex, a genuine smile curving his lips and warming his eyes. "I mean that. You've got great friends."

Alex relaxed slightly. He hadn't realized how worried he'd been about Finn not getting along with his childhood friends until they'd parked outside Hunter's place. For some reason, Alex felt it was important that Finn accepted his friends and vice versa. As to what exactly that reason was, Alex wasn't sure he was ready to explore it yet.

"But? I'm sensing a but," Alex muttered when Finn turned onto the private road that led to the estate.

Finn did not answer right away. Alex waited patiently while they headed through the gates and onto the drive. Finn finally pulled up outside the house and turned the engine off. He turned in his seat to face Alex, his eyes dark and serious.

"Is Drake your ex-lover?"

Alex stiffened. That was not what he'd been expecting Finn to say.

"What makes you think that?" he murmured.

Finn rubbed the back of his neck, lips twisting in an awkward grimace. "I saw the way he looked at you. And I can tell you were ill at ease around him. Tristan said you used to be close in the past."

Alex tried not to squirm in his seat. He wasn't sure he liked where this conversation was going. Talking to Finn about Drake made him feel strangely guilty. That thought brought him up short.

Wait. What do I have to feel guilty about? I haven't done anything wrong.

"Was it a bad breakup?" Finn asked gruffly.

Alex hesitated. It didn't look like Finn was going to let this go.

"No. We parted on good terms." He sighed. "It's only been like that between us since I got back. Drake seems angry with me for some reason."

Lines furrowed Finn's brow. "You mean, since he's found out about us?"

Alex shrugged, still at a loss to understand Drake's behavior. "I think so. Though I don't know why it should."

A muscle jumped in Finn's jawline. "I can hazard a guess."

Alex stared at him, puzzled.

"He's jealous," Finn said in a hard voice.

Alex drew a sharp breath. "What?!"

"Drake is jealous," Finn repeated. "I think even Tristan realizes it."

Alex shook his head violently, his pulse suddenly racing. "No way! Drake never wanted a serious relationship with me in the first place, so why the hell would he be jealous about who I'm going out with now?"

Alex faltered and bit his lip, conscious that he and Finn had yet to discuss what it was exactly that they were to one another.

If Finn noticed Alex's faux pas, he didn't comment on it. "Whatever may have happened between the two of you in the past doesn't change the fact that Drake still wants you."

"Well, I don't, so nothing's gonna happen between us!" Alex snapped.

Something that looked a lot like relief filled Finn's eyes. "You mean that?"

Alex nodded. Finn leaned across the console and kissed him. Heat flashed through Alex when Finn probed his lips with his tongue, seeking entrance. He opened his mouth, his hands finding Finn's nape.

Finn deepened the kiss and shifted closer, his

breathing growing heavy and his tongue meeting Alex's in a bold dance that sent desire rushing through Alex's veins.

Finn groaned and broke the kiss. He pressed his forehead against Alex's, his eyes bright with passion. "Let's get inside."

They left a trail of clothes all the way from the foyer to their room.

Alex's cock throbbed when Finn pushed him down on their bed and knelt on the mattress. Finn yanked Alex's briefs off his legs, his mouth growing busy on Alex's throat and chest while his large hands left a fiery trail on Alex's skin, his fingers touching Alex as if he were one of his sculptures. Alex reached up and undid Finn's jeans, movements jerky with the same lust filling Finn's face.

Finn let out a sexy groan when Alex freed his erection from its overtight confines. He stilled Alex's fingers with one hand and closed his eyes, his breathing ragged and loud. The look in his heated gaze when he opened them again had Alex's heart thudding erratically against his ribs.

"I want to make love to you," Finn said huskily.

Alex grinned. "Isn't that what we're doing?" He lifted off the mattress and nipped Finn's lower lip playfully with his teeth.

Finn cradled Alex's chin in his strong fingers and pressed the softest kiss to his mouth. "I mean, really make love to you," he murmured against Alex's lips, his hot gaze boring into Alex's. "I want to enter you, Alex."

Alex sucked in air when Finn nudged a powerful

knee between his thighs, spreading his legs open. Finn lowered a hand and trailed a thumb along the taut stretch of skin under Alex's shivering balls. Alex's breath hitched when Finn's callused pad found his back passage.

"Here," Finn said, his voice thick with desire. "I want *in* here, Alex."

Alex shuddered when Finn gently stroked the tight folds of his pucker. "*Ah!*"

Finn smiled against Alex's mouth. "Was that a yes?"

Alex gazed at Finn dazedly, his head spinning as all the blood in his body rushed south. "Are you sure? 'Cause if you back out halfway, I think I might just—"

"I won't," Finn promised. "Trust me."

He circled Alex's hole teasingly with his thumb and drew a moan from Alex.

"I've been dreaming about this for days." Finn dipped his head and kissed Alex's throat. "About how badly I want to put my cock inside you. About how hot and tight your ass would feel around me when I fuck you." He opened his mouth and bit down gently on Alex's skin. "Squeezing me. Milking me until I'm bone dry."

Alex hissed in pleasure, his dick jerking out a trail of precum at the torrid picture Finn was painting with his filthy words. He gasped when Finn probed his entrance with the tip of his thumb.

Alex grabbed Finn's hand. "Let me—" he paused and swallowed, "let me shower first."

"Okay," Finn agreed reluctantly.

CHAPTER EIGHTEEN

Finn glanced from the closed bathroom door to the box of condoms and the bottle of lube on the nightstand. His cheeks warmed when he recalled his trip into town and the curious look he'd received from the check-out clerk where he'd purchased the items.

Had someone told him a month ago that he would one day be buying products so he could have sexual intercourse with his hot husband, Finn would have told them to pull the other one.

Yet, as he sat nervously on their bed, his dick and balls throbbing painfully between his thighs while the man he was about to make love to prepared his body for the act, Finn realized that everything he and Alex had done since the day he'd kissed the lawyer in the kitchen had been leading to this moment.

A smile twisted Finn's lips as he glanced at his erect, leaking cock.

And what a moment it is.

Finn knew tonight would be the first time he was truly going to have sex. That it wouldn't be with the woman he had married, or any other woman for that matter, had long ceased to surprise him. He couldn't wait to get inside Alex.

A frown furrowed his brow as he listened to the sound of running water from the next room. He waited another minute before climbing off the bed and going in search of the man he wanted very much to fuck right now.

The sight that met Finn's eyes when he opened the bathroom door and walked inside the steam-filled room almost had him cursing out loud.

Alex stood under the open rain shower, his back to Finn and a hand braced against the dark gray tiles while he worked his ass with the other. The lawyer didn't notice Finn at first, so intent was he on probing and stretching his hole, his pants barely audible above the sound of the water cascading over him.

Finn swallowed as he watched Alex thrust two fingers briskly into his back passage, his hips bumping his erection against the tiles. A shiver raced through Alex when he brought a third finger against the tight rim of his ass.

Finn swore and stormed inside the shower.

Alex startled and looked over his shoulder. "Finn? What are you—"

He gasped, his fingers slipping out of his body as Finn stepped under the pounding water and crowded him against the wall.

Finn growled and plastered his front against Alex's

back. He grabbed Alex's wrists and yanked them above his head, holding them prisoner with one large hand. Alex moaned when Finn's throbbing shaft nudged his butt crack. Finn punched his hips and rubbed the head of his cock against Alex's ass, so close to losing his load he had to bite his lip hard.

"Finn!" Alex trembled and pushed back against Finn.

Finn slipped a hand between their bodies and found Alex's entrance.

Alex hissed when Finn pressed against his hole.

Finn looked down and shuddered when he saw his finger disappear inside Alex. The muscles guarding Alex's ass clamped around him, trapping him in velvety, soft heat.

Fuck. He feels incredible.

"More!" Alex begged. He arched his back and thrust his butt hungrily against Finn's hand.

Finn pressed his mouth to Alex's nape and kissed and sucked his hot flesh while he slipped a second finger inside him.

Alex shivered, forehead dropping against the tiles and legs shifting to give Finn better access to his opening. A long, low sexy sound escaped him when Finn slowly withdrew his fingers and slid them back inside.

Finn's cock ached as he started finger fucking Alex, the feel of Alex's tight passage making him light headed with desire. Alex's gasps and moans rose in volume, matching the rising pace of Finn's hand.

"Finn! *More!*"

Finn cursed and brought a third finger into play. Alex grunted and rose on his tip toes when Finn carefully stretched his pulsing entrance.

Finn paused and kissed Alex's ear. "Are you okay?"

"Yes!" Alex moaned. "It feels—*God*, Finn, it feels *so* good!"

Finn groaned and gave Alex what he so desperately wanted, plundering his hole with his slick fingers, preparing him for what they were about to do. His fingertips traced a small bump inside Alex's back passage as Alex arched his hips.

"*Ah!*"

Finn swore when Alex spasmed violently around his fingers. "Is that your prostate?"

"*Hmmm!*" Alex hummed, nodding jerkily.

Finn's heart thundered in his chest as he thrust his fingers inside Alex and repeatedly stroked and rubbed the bump, Alex's pleasure-filled cries loud in his ears.

Alex came a moment later, his cock exploding all over the tiles while his hips pushed and pumped back erratically against Finn's hand.

Finn waited until Alex's convulsions subsided and his ass stopped twitching before carefully slipping his fingers out. Alex shuddered and swayed where he stood. Finn looped a strong arm around Alex's waist, steadying him. He took hold of Alex's chin and turned his head to take his mouth in a hungry kiss.

Alex's pleasure-glazed eyes met Finn's. "Take me to bed, Finn."

❧

ALEX'S HEART RACED AS FINN GRABBED HIS HAND AND tugged him out of the shower, his breathing still ragged from the intense orgasm Finn had just given him. He glanced at Finn's engorged cock and tugged his lip between his teeth, his ass throbbing at the thought of it buried deep inside his body.

Finn dried them both briskly with a towel before backing Alex out of the bathroom and into the bedroom, his mouth busy on Alex's. Alex's eyes widened when he spied the condoms and lube on the nightstand. He wrenched his mouth from Finn's.

"Where did you get those from?"

"I went into town a few days ago," Finn confessed, nipping at Alex's jawline with his teeth.

Alex took hold of Finn's shoulders and pulled back slightly, more than a little stunned. "You went into town just to buy those?"

Finn arched an eyebrow. "Yeah, I did. You got a problem with that?"

Alex chuckled at Finn's defensive tone. "Nope. I was trying to imagine the look on the face of the check-out clerk you bought them from." A gasp left him when Finn pushed him down on the bed.

"She was curious," Finn said. "Like she was wondering who I was going to use them with."

Goosebumps prickled Alex's skin when Finn raked his body with his scorching gaze.

"What do you suppose she'd think if she could see us right now?"

Alex swallowed a groan as Finn hovered above him and trailed a lazy hand from the pulse throbbing at the base of Alex's throat, all the way down his chest and belly to his stirring cock. Alex flushed.

He couldn't believe he was getting hard again so soon after his orgasm.

Finn's eyes grew molten with desire when he registered Alex's growing erection. He reached for the box of condoms, ripped a foil open with his teeth, and sheathed his trembling shaft.

Alex grabbed a pillow and positioned it under his ass.

"It'll make it easier," he breathed at Finn's questioning look.

Finn leaned down and kissed him passionately before taking the lube from the nightstand.

A familiar scent hit Alex's nostrils when Finn uncapped the bottle and poured a generous amount of the liquid onto his cock and in his hand. "Strawberries?"

Finn paused. "You don't like it?"

Alex smiled and shook his head. "I love it. In fact, I'm going to pour that on you later and blow you."

"Fuck." Finn reached down and clamped a hand around the base of his dick, his expression feral.

Alex shuffled closer to Finn and hooked his legs around Finn's waist. He angled his hips and stretched his entrance enticingly open with his fingers.

"That's what I'm waiting for, so hurry and come in here!"

Finn made an animal sound, grabbed Alex's thigh, and thrust two lubed fingers inside Alex's hole. Alex arched and gripped the bedsheets as Finn started fucking his ass briskly, his fingertips seeking and finding Alex's prostate over and over again. Alex bore the sweet torment for a minute before grabbing hold of Finn's wrist.

"Now, Finn!" he implored, not caring how desperate he sounded. "Please, I want you!"

Finn yanked his fingers out of Alex's body, positioned the tip of his cock against Alex's pulsing entrance, and pushed inside in a single, hard thrust.

Alex's shocked shout was echoed by Finn's guttural groan of satisfaction. Alex grabbed Finn's biceps and panted through his nose. He bit down on his lip while his body slowly accommodated to Finn's thick shaft, his insides burning with the force of Finn's penetration.

"I'm sorry," Finn said stiffly, one hand braced next to Alex's head while the other gripped Alex's hip. "Did I hurt you?"

Alex shook his head and licked the sweat beading his upper lip. He could tell Finn was struggling to maintain his composure.

Alex clenched his fingers on Finn's arms. "You can move," he whispered tremulously.

Finn kept his gaze locked on Alex's and slowly withdrew before sliding back inside. Alex moaned as Finn filled him to the hilt, stretching him deliciously open all over again.

Finn looked down to where their bodies connected intimately and repeated the movement. "So good," he breathed, pleasure darkening his eyes and thickening his voice. "*Fuck*, Alex. It feels so good inside you!"

Alex's heart stuttered when Finn lowered his head and took his mouth in a soft, reverent kiss, his hips pumping his dick rhythmically in and out of Alex's passage.

The kiss soon turned hot and Finn's thrusts fast and hard as he surrendered to passion. The sound of the rocking bed and their heated gasps and groans soon filled Alex's world until all that existed was the man who was possessing him with a wildness that made his heart melt with more than just desire.

Blood roared in Alex's ears as his orgasm built in slow waves, tightening his lower body like a bow. Finn growled and rose above him, his hips growing erratic as he too neared his own climax.

Alex fisted his shaft, eager to come with the man making love to him. A tortured moan escaped him when Finn closed his hand over his own. Alex gazed into Finn's eyes where he moved above him and grasped his intent. He let go, surrendering control to Finn.

Finn's face twisted in a savage mask of ecstasy as he gave Alex's cock several brisk strokes and took Alex over the edge with him.

Whiteness bloomed behind Alex's eyelids, his cries of pleasure and Finn's feral grunts reaching him dimly above the sound of blood roaring in his ears. His passage pulsed and spasmed repeatedly around Finn's throbbing shaft while his dick jetted out stream after stream of hot cum onto his belly.

Finn's weight pressed Alex into the mattress when he collapsed onto him a moment later, his face coming to rest in the crook of Alex's neck. Alex wrapped his arms around Finn and sank in the afterglow of their lovemaking, aftershocks of pleasure still coursing through him. He let out a soft sound of protest when Finn slipped out of him, his body feeling suddenly bereft. Finn disposed of the condom before taking Alex into his arms and kissing him tenderly.

Alex's heart swelled with happiness as he looked into Finn's sated eyes.

"Was that good?" he murmured against Finn's lips.

Finn bumped his nose against Alex's. "That was more than good," he said fervently. "You just rocked my world, Alex Hancock."

Alex smiled.

"What are you thinking about?" Finn murmured.

Alex chuckled. "I'm thinking it's a good thing Aunt Maggie never had cameras installed in here."

Finn's eyes widened with a mixture of shock and curious excitement.

Alex grinned when he felt Finn's cock stir against his thigh. He grabbed the bottle of lube from the nightstand, dropped a kiss on Finn's lips, and shuffled down the bed.

"Now, about that thing I said I wanted to do earlier."

CHAPTER NINETEEN

Finn opened his eyes languidly. Light washed through the glass wall of the bedroom, filling the space with warm brightness. He stretched and started to roll onto his back.

An arm tightened possessively around his waist.

Finn stilled and looked down.

Alex was tucked against his body, one leg draped carelessly across Finn's thighs while he hugged Finn in his sleep.

Finn's chest swelled with emotion. He lifted a hand and ran a knuckle gently down Alex's cheek, unable to resist touching him again, even though that was all he'd done last night.

Touch him. Kiss him. Blow him. Fuck him.

Finn's body heated up as he recalled how hungrily he'd made love to Alex. He'd never thought of himself as being aggressive in bed or having a particularly high libido but, like with everything else he'd experienced with Alex since that fateful kiss, his expectations of his

131

own sexuality and his physical needs had been blown right out of the water last night.

Finn had never felt the desire to possess someone as badly as he'd done Alex. To take him so hard and deep he thought he would carve his very shape inside his body. To make him beg and moan and scream with a pleasure only Finn could give him. To watch him shatter over and over again.

Alex had not only fulfilled all of Finn's filthiest desires, he'd done so with a passion that equaled Finn's, his kisses and touches filled with the same burning urgency that had consumed Finn. The way Alex had responded to Finn told Finn this was more than just sex for Alex too.

The lawyer sighed in his sleep as Finn caressed his cheek again. He shifted a little closer, blindly seeking Finn's touch. Finn swallowed a groan when the covers slipped from Alex's waist and exposed the sweet curve of his naked hip and butt.

Finn's cock stirred as he imagined climbing onto Alex and slipping into the tight, hot passage that had gripped and milked his dick so splendidly last night. He slipped a hand down his body and grasped his growing erection with a grimace.

If we make love again, he's not gonna be able to walk. He paused. *On the other hand...*

Finn was entertaining the idea of going under the covers and blowing Alex awake when the distant sound of the doorbell reached him. He frowned and looked over his shoulder.

The clock on the nightstand indicated it was early

afternoon. He wasn't expecting any visitors and, as far as he knew, neither was Alex.

A pair of sleepy blue eyes met Finn's gaze when he turned around.

"'Morning," Alex murmured.

Finn's cock throbbed at Alex's croaky voice. He knew he was to blame for Alex's hoarseness. He leaned in and gave Alex the kiss he'd been dying to give him since he'd woken up. Alex slipped his arms around Finn's neck and lazily opened his lips, welcoming Finn inside.

The doorbell chimed again.

Alex blinked at Finn fuzzily before wrenching their mouths apart. "You expecting someone?"

"No." Finn sighed and reluctantly rolled out of bed. He grabbed his pajama bottoms and was slipping into them when Alex blew out a dreamy sigh.

"Is it bad that I want to come over there and sink my teeth in your butt?" the lawyer mumbled, desire darkening his eyes. He pushed the covers off his body and lowered his hand to clasp his swelling erection.

Finn groaned. "Don't. Otherwise I'm going to climb back in that bed and inside you."

Alex grinned, bent one knee, and gave Finn a glimpse of the shadowy space under his balls while he stroked himself, his cheeks flushing the same rosy pink as his dick.

"Why don't you get rid of whoever is at the door and come back and do that?" Alex tugged at his leaking cock and dipped his fingers lower.

Finn clenched his jaw when Alex started

deliberately playing with his ass, his hot blue gaze locked unblinkingly on Finn's. Teasing him. Taunting him.

"Give me a minute!" Finn growled and stormed out of the bedroom.

Alex's throaty chuckle followed him down the corridor and the stairs. Finn collected the items of clothing they'd scattered through the house, bunched them in one hand, and yanked the front door open just as the doorbell chimed for the third time.

"Yes?" Finn snapped impatiently.

His stomach dropped when he saw the figure on his doorstep.

Aunt Maggie blinked at him. Her eyes widened when she took in his disheveled appearance. They gravitated to the clothes in his hand.

A light Finn didn't like the look of lit up Aunt Maggie's face. "Good afternoon, Finn."

ALEX SHRUGGED A T-SHIRT OVER HIS HEAD AND PADDED out of the bedroom. It had been ten minutes since Finn had woken him up with a sinfully hot kiss and left him with a hard-on that he hadn't returned to assuage.

The sound of voices reached Alex's ears when he neared the stairs. He frowned.

It was clear Finn hadn't been able to get rid of their visitor.

Alex negotiated the mezzanine and came in sight of the living room. He froze on the spiral steps when he saw the two people who turned to watch him from where they sat on the couch.

"Hi, Alex," Finn's aunt greeted with a knowing smile. "It's good to see you again. I'm sorry I haven't visited since the wedding."

Finn looked pale where he sat next to his aunt. Alex quelled the uneasy feeling blooming inside him at the haunted expression in Finn's eyes and took the rest of the stairs at a steady pace.

"Aunt Maggie." Alex closed the distance to the couch and pressed a light kiss to Finn's aunt's cheek. He glanced at Finn, his tone relaxed. "Shall I make us some tea?"

Aunt Maggie beamed. "Tea would be great."

By the time Alex returned to the room with a tray loaded with a teapot and three cups, he was convinced Finn had started to regret what had happened between them last night. It was clear from Finn's behavior that he didn't want his aunt to find out about them. Pain twisted Alex's heart at that thought.

"I must say, you boys look terribly peaky considering it's such a lovely afternoon," Aunt Maggie said, taking a sip of the tea Alex had poured her. "Are you okay?"

"We're fine, thank you," Finn said, not meeting Alex's eyes. "Did you need something?"

Aunt Maggie studied Finn with an innocent expression. "Can't an old lady come say hello to her favorite nephew?"

Finn sighed. "You normally call before you drop by."

"Well, I wanted to surprise you," Aunt Maggie said a

tad defensively. She glanced at Alex. "And I wanted to see how things were going between the two of you."

"Things are good, thanks," Finn said stiffly.

"I see." Aunt Maggie's shrewd eyes moved from Finn to Alex and back again. "Is there anything you wish to tell me?"

A muscle jumped in Finn's cheek. His expression grew stormy as he studied his aunt's expectant expression.

"Did Izzy say something to you?"

Alex's heart thumped when he registered the genuine anger in Finn's eyes.

Finn rose to his feet, came over to Alex's armchair, and sat on the arm rest. He reached down and clasped Alex's hand firmly in his own.

Alex gazed at him, startled.

"About us?" Finn added in a hard voice.

Aunt Maggie slowly lowered her cup to the coffee table, her expression growing serious. "No, she didn't."

Blood thundered in Alex's veins as he blinked dazedly at Finn.

Wait. So, he doesn't *regret what happened between us?*

Finn met his shocked stare. Alex drew a shaky breath when he saw the light blazing in Finn's eyes.

"Alex and I —" Finn paused, his throat working, "Alex and I are going out." He gazed defiantly at his aunt. "I don't know where this will lead, but—" He faltered.

"But we want this." Alex clenched his fingers around Finn's and turned to face his aunt. "Right now, we want to be together."

The words they had yet to say to one another resonated in the tense silence that fell across the room.

Tears filled Aunt Maggie's eyes. "Thank God," she said huskily.

Alex glanced at Finn, alarmed. The same confusion he was experiencing was reflected on the artist's face.

Aunt Maggie sniffed, pulled a handkerchief from her handbag, and dabbed at her eyes. "You've finally accepted it, haven't you?"

"Accepted what?" Finn mumbled.

"Your sexuality."

Finn's hand trembled around Alex's. "How did you —" He stopped, too shaken up to speak.

Aunt Maggie's expression softened. "I've suspected it for a long time."

CHAPTER TWENTY

FINN STEELED HIMSELF FOR THE INEVITABLE GUILT THAT would storm his heart at his aunt's shocking words. Except, there was none. All he felt was the most incredible sense of relief. He blinked, surprised.

Is this what Alex experienced when he came out to his family? This—this feeling of freedom?

"I suspected you were gay long before Catherine came to me with her suspicions," Aunt Maggie continued.

A buzzing noise filled Finn's ears. "What?" he said numbly.

"Catherine thought you were gay," Aunt Maggie said gently. "We spoke about it on many an occasion."

"I—" Finn paused and closed his eyes for a moment, not quite believing what he was hearing.

His aunt's voice was devoid of any accusation as she continued talking.

"All I ever wanted was for you to be happy, Finn. As did Catherine. She told me this even in the last days of her illness." A wry smile curved Aunt Maggie's lips. "Forcing you into this fake marriage wasn't just my idea, you know. Catherine wanted you to be able to open your heart to someone after her death, so she asked me to do something about it if ever the opportunity arose." She paused. "To be honest, when Izzy called me and told me what you'd said about not really caring what the sex of the person you would marry was, I thought it would be a perfect opportunity to test my and Catherine's theories. And when Izzy brought Alex into the picture, it seemed like fate." Her eyes gleamed with wetness as she looked from Finn to Alex. "I'm happy for you. And Catherine would be too, Finn."

Tears blurred Finn's vision as he gazed at the woman who had raised him. "Thank you."

Aunt Maggie left a short while later. Finn closed the front door after her and turned to see Alex watching him with a quiet intensity.

"Did you mean what you said?" the lawyer asked in a low voice. "About the two of us going out?"

Finn closed the distance to Alex and took his hand. "Yes." He stared at Alex. "What about you? Did you mean it when you said you wanted to be with me?"

Alex tilted his chin and met Finn's eyes unflinchingly. "Yes."

Finn raised Alex's hand to his mouth and dropped a hot kiss on his knuckles. Alex wrapped his arms around Finn's waist and pressed his face to Finn's throat, his body trembling slightly in Finn's hold.

"I know now that my impotency had everything to

do with my suppressed sexuality," Finn admitted quietly in Alex's hair. "I loved Catherine. But it was the love of a man toward his best friend and not that of a man enamored with his life partner. What I feel for you is…different."

Alex stayed quiet for some time, his heart thumping strongly against Finn's chest.

"You know, we've done things completely the wrong way around," he murmured.

Finn pulled back and studied him with a faint smile. "How so?"

"First, we got married. Then, we kissed. After that came handjobs and blowjobs. And finally, we had sex last night." Alex chuckled. "We seriously missed out on the dating phase."

Finn grinned. "Are you asking me out on a date, Hancock?"

Alex arched an eyebrow. "I will if you're nice to me."

Finn laughed, enjoying this game. "And what can I do to be—" he brought his lips to Alex's ear, "nice to you?"

Alex shivered as Finn's breath washed across his skin. "Well, you can start by taking me back to upstairs and doing what you promised to do to me an hour ago."

Alex's delighted laughter rang in Finn's ears as Finn grabbed his hand and tugged him toward the stairs.

It was evening by the time they got out of bed and showered.

"Wanna head into town?" Alex said, rubbing his hair with a towel.

"Sure," Finn replied with a smile.

Alex grinned. "How about you ride on the back of my bike? I have a spare helmet?"

"Well, considering I've been riding you most of last night and today, I'd say hell yes," Finn drawled.

He chuckled when Alex rolled his eyes hard at him.

They ended up having dinner at a small Italian restaurant. Though the place was busy and they earned themselves some curious stares, Finn found himself not caring. All he wanted to do was spend time with the alluring man who had bewitched him body and mind.

They stepped out into the cool night air a couple of hours later and strolled to where Alex had parked the Triumph.

"Do you want to get a drink before we head back?" Alex asked.

"Sure," Finn murmured.

He and Catherine had never been to any of the bars in town since they moved to Twilight Falls. He was kind of curious to see what kind of place Alex liked to visit.

They pulled up outside a pretty gray and white clapboard building on the other side of town a short while later. Finn climbed off the back of the Triumph and removed his helmet. He stared at the bright pink neon sign above the door of the establishment.

"'The Watering Hole'?" Finn looked at Alex. "Is this somewhere you used to hang out before you left Twilight Falls?"

"I left Twilight Falls when I was eighteen, so not

exactly the age to be visiting bars," Alex drawled. "Hunter and Tristan told me about this place."

To Finn's surprise, the bar was packed. His eyes widened when he observed the predominantly male clientele filling the booths and perched at high tables. The beats of a popular pop song thrummed through Finn's boots as he followed Alex through the crowd. He gazed toward the back of the building and caught a glimpse of a raised floor crowned with a glittering disco ball.

"Wait," he hissed to Alex as they made their way to the bar. "Is this a—a gay club?!"

Alex flashed him a grin over his shoulder. "Kinda. They don't advertise it as such. But it gets plenty of male visitors from the surrounding towns."

They'd just ordered a beer and a soda when a familiar face appeared next to them.

"Hey, you two," Wyatt greeted.

Finn stiffened when he saw the man behind Wyatt.

Drake dipped his chin at Finn. "Hi."

"Hi," Finn murmured in return.

Alex turned and startled slightly when he saw Drake. He greeted the two men with a nod. "Hey."

"Care to join us?" Wyatt said. "Hunter and Tristan are trying to find us somewhere to sit."

Finn exchanged a glance with Alex.

Alex hesitated before shrugging. "Sure."

They ended up at a table next to the window.

"So, how are you two lovebirds doing?" Hunter looked from Finn to Alex and tipped his beer to his lips, a grin pasted across his face.

"We were having a great time until you guys turned up," Alex said.

Finn masked a smile at the lawyer's tart tone. He could tell Alex had wanted them to spend some more private time together.

"Oh." Hunter's expression radiated innocence. "Did we interrupt your *date*?"

Alex narrowed his eyes.

Finn chuckled. "You did, actually." He looped an arm around Alex's waist and gazed at the surprised men staring at them. "I was just getting to know my rather hot husband."

Alex arched an arrogant eyebrow. "I'm sorry, did you just say 'rather'?"

Finn laughed. "Okay, uber. Like, seriously hot."

"That's better," Alex said with a cocky smile.

Finn caught Drake's faint frown. He ignored the flash of jealous possessiveness that darted through him and swallowed a sip of his beer.

"So, does the fact that you're here mean you're all gay?" Finn indicated their surroundings.

Wyatt smiled wryly. "Pretty much."

"And you've been friends since you were kids?" Finn asked, his interest piqued.

"Yup," Hunter said with a nod.

"And you guys have never—" Finn waved a hand at them vaguely, "you know?"

Wyatt raised an eyebrow. "Slept with one another? Bar Drake and Alex, no."

Hunter choked on his drink. Tristan grimaced and patted him on the back as he coughed and spluttered.

"What?!" Hunter blurted out when he could talk again. He stared from Wyatt, to Drake and Alex. "*You two slept with each other?!*"

"Your powers of observation never cease to amaze me," Tristan told Hunter drily.

Alex ignored them and frowned at Wyatt. "When did you find out?"

Wyatt shrugged laconically. "On the night you turned sixteen."

Alex's eyes widened. He flushed in the next instant. "Wait. Does that mean you—"

"I got up to go to the restroom in the middle of the night," Wyatt said. "Your house has thin walls."

Alex groaned and covered his face with his hands.

A sinking feeling filled the pit of Finn's stomach as he looked from Alex, to Wyatt and Drake.

Drake watched Finn with an inscrutable expression.

By the time they got on the Triumph and rode home, Finn knew his suspicions were correct. He buried his face in Alex's back, his hands clenching on Alex's windbreaker.

Not only was Drake Alex's former lover, he was also the man who had taken Alex's virginity.

CHAPTER TWENTY-ONE

"It's beautiful." Izzy stared at the sculpture that would soon form the central piece of Finn's upcoming art exhibition, her green eyes bright with excitement. "It's you and Alex, isn't it?"

Finn studied the sensuous lines of the alabaster creation he'd spent the last two weeks creating. It was one of the best pieces he'd ever made and he knew he owed it all to the man who had captivated his body and soul these past weeks.

"Is it that obvious?"

Izzy shook her head. "Only to someone who knows what's going on between you." She crossed the studio and took Finn's hand. "I'm happy for you. I mean that, Finn."

A lump formed in Finn's throat at Izzy's sincere tone. "Thank you."

The exhibition was only ten days away and Finn was busy putting the finishing touches to the last pieces of his collection. Izzy had come to the studio to take pictures of the artwork that would feature in the display.

"Where's Alex, by the way?" Izzy asked as she put her camera away.

Finn smiled. "Down by the creek. I wouldn't let him see this piece until the night of the exhibition, so he's sulking."

"That's cruel. He posed for you, right?"

"Yeah. But this piece is…special. And I want him to see it in the best possible lighting."

Finn's ears grew warm as he looked around the studio and recalled the long, sensual hours he and Alex had spent in this room. Having Alex model for him had turned out to be a great idea not just for his creativity, but for his libido too.

Izzy wrinkled her nose at him. "Jeez, you guys made out in here, didn't you? Like in that movie about that man who died and became a ghost?"

Finn chuckled at the classic reference. "I would love to say that we were that refined, but we weren't."

Izzy rolled her eyes. She left a while later, with the promise of sending Finn the photographs she'd taken for his final approval. Finn spent another hour finalizing the piece he'd been working on and finally went in search of Alex.

Over a week had passed since his encounter with Alex's friends at The Watering Hole. Although Finn hadn't questioned Alex about whether Drake was the one who'd taken his virginity before he left Twilight Falls, his gut instinct told him he was right on the money.

The fact that Drake was Alex's first man shouldn't have bothered Finn so much. Except it did. And Finn realized this spoke volumes of his feelings for the lawyer.

He found Alex sitting on a boulder in the creek, his bare feet dangling in the water.

"Isn't it cold?"

Alex looked around at Finn's voice. He shook his head. "It's pretty nice, actually." He glanced past Finn. "Has Izzy left?"

"Uh-huh." Finn kicked his shoes off, climbed on the boulder, and dropped down next to Alex. He rolled the hems of his jeans before dipping his feet in the water. "You're right. This feels great."

Silence fell between them.

"So, you still sulking?" Finn asked in a light tone.

Alex narrowed his eyes at him. "Are you seriously not going to let me see your central piece until the night of the exhibition?"

Finn grinned. "Nope. I want it to be a surprise."

Suspicion filled Alex's eyes. "It had better not be a giant sculpture of my dick. I won't be able to show my face in town if it is."

Finn chuckled at that. "No, it isn't." He paused and rubbed his chin, his expression teasing. "Although, that's not a bad idea."

He laughed when Alex tried to push him into the water.

"You know, I don't think I'll put out tonight," Alex grumbled.

Finn raised an eyebrow. "What? No sex? Are you

sure? 'Cause I made you moan pretty loud last night and I suspect you might like a repeat."

Alex stuck his tongue out at Finn.

Finn swooped in and took Alex's mouth in a kiss that had the lawyer melting in his arms.

"Not fair," Alex mumbled against Finn's lips when Finn ended their kiss long seconds later. His cheeks were flushed and his eyes indigo with desire as he clung to Finn.

"All's fair in love and war," Finn murmured with a grin.

Alex blinked, surprise dilating his pupils.

Finn stiffened slightly when he realized what he'd just said.

Shit.

Alex tilted his head to one side. "Is that so?"

Finn hesitated before nodding, knowing he couldn't be anything but honest with Alex right now. "Uh-huh."

Alex watched him for a while longer. "I have a question for you."

A mixture of relief and disappointment danced through Finn. Relief that Alex hadn't questioned him about the nature of his feelings. Disappointment that he didn't know what Alex felt for him either.

"What's the question?"

Alex took Finn's hand and linked their fingers together. "Have you ever made love in a river?"

Finn gasped when Alex tugged on his arm and jumped in the creek. They landed with a splash, their feet sinking into the soft, gravelly bottom while the water lapped at their thighs.

Alex laughed at Finn's stunned expression. "You should see the look on your face!"

Finn narrowed his eyes, scooped water in his hands, and splashed Alex in the face.

Alex spluttered and sucked in air, outraged. "Oh, you're *asking* for it, West!"

By the time they finished their water fight, they were both soaked through and Finn was more than a little aroused.

Water gleamed in Alex's hair and on his eyelashes and lips. His wet clothes clung enticingly to his body, highlighting his nipples, his washboard abs, and his strong, tanned legs.

He's so beautiful.

Finn's cock stirred when he saw Alex's growing erection. "Come here."

Alex closed the distance between them, his eyes feverish with desire.

Finn grabbed Alex's waist and plastered their bodies together before taking Alex's mouth in a hungry kiss. Alex moaned and speared Finn's wet hair with desperate fingers, his tongue meeting Finn's ardently.

Finn lowered his hands to Alex's butt and backed him to the closest boulder, his pulse racing and his cock doing press-ups behind the zipper of his jeans. Alex gasped when Finn lifted him to sit on the edge of the rock. Finn leaned in and sucked Alex's nipples through the see-through material of his shirt. Alex hissed in pleasure and clutched the back of Finn's head, his hips bucking. Finn growled and pinched and twisted one hard nub with his fingers while he circled and flicked the other with his tongue. He trailed one hand down Alex's body and undid the buttons of his shorts.

A husky groan left Alex when Finn freed his rigid shaft and palmed his trembling, hot flesh. Finn hastily unbuttoned Alex's shirt and kissed a torrid path down Alex's chest and belly before taking Alex's cock in his mouth, eager to taste him.

Alex leaned his hands on the boulder and dropped his head back. Air left his throat in soft hums and moans as Finn worked his erection slickly with his lips and tongue.

Finn sucked and teased Alex until he exploded with a violent shout, his butt rolling off the rock in deep, hard thrusts as he fucked Finn's mouth. Finn spat out Alex's cum in one hand, clasped his arm, and tugged him back in the water. He stilled for a moment.

Alex's skin was still flushed from his orgasm and his chest rose and fell rapidly with his breathing as he looked dazedly at Finn.

Finn clenched his teeth at the sensuous expression glazing Alex's face, his dick throbbing painfully between his thighs. He grabbed Alex's hip and turned him around.

"Put your hands on the rock, Alex."

Alex obeyed Finn's gruff command and looked at Finn over his shoulder, his blue eyes dark with excitement.

Finn peeled Alex's shorts down and off his legs before casting them on top of the boulder. Alex trembled when Finn parted his buttcheeks and brought his cum-slicked fingers to his entrance.

"Can I, Alex?" Finn murmured in Alex's right ear. He stroked and teased Alex's hole for long seconds before slowly thrusting one finger inside him. "Can I come in here?"

Alex shuddered and pushed back as Finn started finger fucking him at a steady, unhurried pace.

Finn bit down on Alex's earlobe and smiled fiercely when Alex hissed and bucked against him. "Can I fuck you raw, Alex?"

Finn's pulse raced as he waited breathlessly for Alex's answer. He'd been wanting to do this for a while now. To take Alex without the presence of a physical barrier between their bodies. In the end, he'd hesitated and never voiced the filthiest of all his desires, not sure how Alex would react to his request.

But here, now, in this primal moment where they stood surrounded by towering evergreens and cool, clear water, Finn finally felt able to ask the question.

"Yes," Alex breathed. His eyes were indigo pools of desire as he looked back at Finn, the flags of color on his cheekbones telling Finn he wanted this as badly as Finn did. He dropped his head forward and angled his nape, seeking Finn's kiss. "Enter me, Finn!"

Finn made an animal sound and slipped a second finger inside Alex at the same time he bit down on his neck. Alex gasped and tightened around him, his insides sucking Finn greedily. Finn scissored his fingers and stretched Alex, his heart thudding so fast against his ribs he feared it would burst from his chest.

By the time Finn freed his erection and brought the head of his bare cock to Alex's hole, both of them were breathing hard. Alex moaned and rose on his tip toes when Finn pushed inside his body in a slow, long thrust. Finn gripped Alex's hips and stilled, giving Alex time to adjust to his engorged shaft.

He bit his lip hard as his cock throbbed inside Alex. He couldn't believe how hot and tight and velvety soft Alex's body was without the presence of a thin, rubber layer.

Shit. I think I'm gonna come the minute I start to move.

"Finn," Alex begged. He squeezed Finn with his hole, causing Finn to curse. "Please!"

Finn growled and gave Alex what they both wanted so very badly. Water sloshed around them as Finn punched his hips and started fucking Alex, his pace fast and hard from the get go. He looked down to where his cock was disappearing inside Alex's back passage and swore at the sinful sight of Alex's cum slicked hole spasming and dragging along the sensitive skin of his shaft.

Alex spread his legs wide and braced himself, his knuckles whitening on the boulder and his body jolting with Finn's powerful thrusts. Finn bunched the tails of Alex's shirt against his back and reached around to palm Alex's straining cock.

"*Ah!*" Alex gasped.

Finn's orgasm danced down his spine and tightened his balls as he fucked Alex and stroked his dick. He threw his head back and groaned at the clear blue sky, the rush of water and the sigh of wind in the trees a heady backdrop to the animal sounds of his and Alex's lovemaking.

Alex's cock throbbed and pulsed in Finn's grip as his orgasm hit him. He came with a hoarse shout, his insides clenching Finn's shaft so hard Finn swore, his hot cum filling Finn's hand.

The delicious spasms rippling through Alex's ass tipped Finn over the edge. He grasped Alex's waist in a punishing hold and pumped wildly into Alex's back passage, his cock spurting out jet after jet of thick cum inside Alex's body.

Finn dropped his face against Alex's nape and closed his arms around him, his jerking hips gradually slowing to a stop. They stayed like that for a while, Finn's cock wedged deep inside Alex while their breathing returned to normal and their hearts stopped racing.

Alex moaned when Finn slipped out of him.

A hot feeling of possessiveness stormed Finn's heart when he saw his cum trickling down the back of Alex's thigh. He turned Alex around and took his mouth in a heated kiss before grabbing his hand and leading him deeper into the creek.

"Let's clean you up."

CHAPTER TWENTY-TWO

ALEX STEPPED OUT OF THE COURTHOUSE AND TURNED TO shake Casey's hand.

"I'll finalize the paperwork when I get back to the office. With the restraining order now permanent, you'll finally get to see the back of your husband."

Casey smiled, her eyes bright with relief despite her tired expression. "Thank you, Alex. I couldn't have done this without you."

Casey's friend beamed at Alex.

Alex waited until the two women got in their car and drove out of the parking lot before heading back across town. He was climbing the stairs to his office when his cell buzzed in his back pocket. He took it out and froze when he saw the number on the display.

Alex hurried up the rest of the steps, slammed his office door shut behind him, and dropped his bag on the floor. His hand shook as he pressed the answer button.

"Mr. Hancock?" Agent Barnes said briskly on the other end of the line.

Alex's palms grew sweaty. "Yes?"

"We have Ryan Fisher in custody."

A lightheaded feeling swept over Alex. He leaned a hip against his desk to support his trembling legs and looked blindly out of the window. "How did you—"

"His cousin slipped up. We traced a call he made to a public phone and arranged to have the area watched. We picked up Mr. Fischer from a hotel close to that location two hours ago." The agent paused. "There's one more thing. We traced the funds he stole from your business to an account in the Cayman Islands. Most of it is there. Looks like he was waiting for the heat to die down before investing in bonds and property."

Alex's heart pounded against his ribs as the FBI agent's words sank in.

"Are you there, Mr. Hancock?"

"Yeah." Alex swallowed. "Yes, I am. What happens now?"

"We'll be filing charges against Mr. Fischer. He'll appear before a judge in the next few days. You will obviously have to testify against him when the case goes to court. As for the stolen funds, they will be released into your company's accounts after due process."

The call ended with Agent Barnes promising to inform Alex when he would be required to come to San Diego. Alex stared at his cell for a long time before putting it away. He glanced distractedly at his watch.

It was five twenty in the afternoon. He'd promised Finn he'd be home by six.

Alex grabbed his things and headed out of the door, his mind in turmoil. He needed a drink, badly. He slowed as he passed Hunter's shop and briefly considered asking him out, but decided against it.

He needed to be alone right now, to think things through.

With the embezzled funds from his law firm recovered, Alex knew there was no longer any reason for him to continue his sham of a marriage to Finn. Two months ago, he would have been over the moon at this piece of news. Except now, he wasn't.

Alex had just ordered a Bourbon at The Watering Hole when someone slipped onto the bar stool next to him. He stifled a groan.

"Hi," Drake drawled. "You don't seem happy to see me."

"I'm not," Alex muttered. "I really want to be on my own right now."

A frown furrowed Drake's brow as he searched Alex's troubled face. "What's wrong?"

The bartender came over and slid Alex's drink in front of him. "Here you go."

Alex grabbed the glass and took a large gulp of whisky. He hissed when the spirit burned a fiery trail down his throat.

"You don't normally drink whisky," Drake said, concern lacing his voice.

Alex hesitated for a moment before telling Drake

about the phone call he'd received from the FBI a while back and the one he'd just gotten.

Drake's expression cleared. "That's great. This means you can end your fake marriage to Finn."

Alex's heart twisted as Drake voiced his worse fears.

"You don't look happy about that," Drake murmured.

Alex ran a hand through his hair. "I'm not."

"Is that because you're in love with him?" Drake asked, his tone hardening.

Alex's fingers clenched on his glass. "I—"

"I can make you forget him," Drake said. "Come back to me, Alex."

Alex froze when Drake suddenly leaned in and kissed him.

"There you are. I told Finn I saw you head this way and—"

Alex wrenched his mouth free from Drake's and turned to see Hunter gaping at them from the entrance of the bar. His stomach plummeted when his gaze found the man standing frozen next to Hunter.

The color drained from Finn's face. He stared at Alex and Drake as if he'd seen a ghost, his eyes dark with a nameless emotion.

"Finn," Alex mumbled. "This isn't what it looks—"

Finn twisted on his heels and stormed out of the bar.

Hunter gazed at Finn's disappearing back before turning to frown at Alex and Drake. "Would someone care to explain what just happened?"

THE RUMBLE OF ALEX'S TRIUMPH REACHED FINN'S EARS as he paced the living room of their home, his mind a jumbled mess. He hadn't waited to see if Alex would follow him when he'd walked out of The Watering Hole and had gone straight to where he'd parked his Jeep.

Finn couldn't remember driving home. The only thing that kept replaying in front of his eyes was the scene he'd just witnessed.

He'd gone into town to ask Alex out on a special dinner date. There was something he'd been working on the last few days, a secret project that had finally come to fruition that afternoon. Finn had collected the items before making his way to Alex's office, his body wrought with nervous tension.

He was finally ready to tell Alex how he felt about him and he hoped he was right about how Alex would respond to his confession.

He'd headed to Hunter's shop when he'd found Alex's office empty and had followed Hunter to The Watering Hole, eager to see the man who he hoped was about to change his life all over again.

Neither he nor Hunter had expected what they'd witnessed when they'd walked into the bar. That much had been clear from Hunter's reaction.

Finn's mind had gone blank when he'd seen Drake kissing Alex. The only thing he recalled was the sound of his heart pounding violently against his ribs and the roar of blood in his ears, every thump an agonizing beat of despair and loss.

The front door opened and closed with a loud thud. Rapid footsteps sounded in the hallway. Alex appeared on the threshold of the living room. His cheeks were flushed and his expression wild.

They stared at each other in taut silence from across the floor.

"Say something," Alex whispered.

Finn swallowed and bunched his fists at his sides. "What do you want me to say?"

"Something," Alex implored. He took a step toward Finn. "Anything."

Finn watched him close the distance between them, his heart at war with his mind. "How long?"

Alex faltered and stopped at Finn's icy tone. "What?"

Finn finally gave in to the anger surging through him and grabbed the collar of Alex's shirt. "How long have you been sleeping with him?!"

Alex blinked, his face turning pale. "Wait. You think I'm cheating on you? With Drake?!"

"*Can you blame me?!*" Finn roared, body shaking with the strength of the violent emotions threatening to consume him. "What else am I supposed to think, Alex?! I came into town to surprise you and I find you kissing Drake like you two have been—"

"*He* kissed me!" A scowl darkened Alex's face, some of the color returning to his cheeks. "Do you really think so little of me, Finn? Do you honestly believe I would sleep with another man when I'm—" He stopped and swallowed convulsively.

Finn's heart thudded painfully in his chest. "When you're what, Alex?"

Alex closed his eyes briefly. "When I'm in love with you," he confessed in a tremulous voice.

Finn let go of Alex's shirt and took a step back.

The light slowly went out of Alex's eyes at Finn's reaction, the same torment rushing through Finn's veins pasted across his ashen face. "Is that your answer?"

Finn hesitated. "I—" He lapsed into silence, struggling to find the words to express what he was feeling right now.

Alex squared his shoulders, a muscle jumping in his jawline. He twisted on his heels. "I'll send someone to collect my things."

Finn blinked, his thoughts utterly derailed. "What?"

Alex stopped where he was headed out of the room. "The FBI just arrested my former business partner," he said, his back to Finn. "They'd recovered the funds he embezzled. I don't need your money anymore, Finn. And by looks of it, you don't want me in your life." He paused, his voice shaking. "Let me make something crystal clear before I go. Drake was the one who kissed me. And I punched him after you left."

Alex's words echoed painfully in Finn's ears.

"Wait," Finn whispered, his heart breaking all over again. "Are you saying this is over? That *we're* over?"

A harsh bark of laughter escaped Alex. He rubbed

the back of his neck and looked at Finn over his shoulder.

"Well, I can't deny that the sex wasn't great. And I'm glad that I helped you discover your sexual orientation."

Finn's world came crashing down around him when he saw the tears in Alex's eyes.

"But yeah," Alex whispered, "we're over, Finn."

And with that, he stormed out of the house and Finn's life.

CHAPTER TWENTY-THREE

"You need to eat something."

Alex sighed and closed the refrigerator door. "I'm not hungry."

He popped open the can of beer he'd just taken out and took a sip.

Izzy scowled at Wyatt where the two of them sat having dinner at their kitchen table. "Say something to him."

Wyatt rolled the last of his spaghetti onto his fork. "He's a grown man, Izzy. He'll eat when he wants to."

Izzy blew out a frustrated sigh. Guilt pierced Alex at the worried light in her eyes.

It had been two days since he'd turned up on Izzy and Wyatt's doorstep. Though Izzy had been upset when he'd told her what had happened between Finn and him, she'd agreed to fetch his clothes from Finn's place yesterday. Wyatt told Alex she'd also stormed off to Drake's place to give him a piece of her mind.

"Hunter said you punched Drake after he kissed you," Wyatt had muttered, amusement lacing his words. "Izzy said Drake had quite the shiner. It's worrying how happy she seemed about that fact."

"Well, he deserved it," Alex had mumbled irately.

"So, you're really thinking of going back to San Diego?" Izzy asked presently, a mournful look in her eyes.

"I—" Alex faltered. "I haven't made up my mind yet."

Wyatt put his fork down and gazed at Alex. "You could stay in Twilight Falls. Expand your business here." A melancholic smile crossed his lips. "We'll miss you if you go, Alex."

Alex was still mulling over Wyatt's words when he stepped outside the back door a few hours later. It was after midnight and he couldn't sleep. He sat on the porch swing and set it rocking gently while he gazed at the starlit sky, his mind and heart as troubled as they had been the day he walked out of Finn's home.

Finn's accusation had hurt Alex more than he thought it would. The fact that Finn hadn't trusted him had haunted Alex's every waking moment since that awful night.

But more than that, it was Finn's reaction to Alex's confession that had crushed his fragile heart. Because confessing his feelings for Finn, laying his soul bare to the man he wanted to be with for the rest of his life, had taken all of Alex's courage in the moment when he'd said those words.

Alex knew that Finn cherished him. And he'd been

willing to wait for as long as it took to hear the words he so very much wanted Finn to say to him.

I guess that won't happen now.

Emotion clogged Alex's throat at that thought. His fingers clenched into fists in his lap.

Movement to the right drew his gaze. A figure appeared around the side of the house.

Alex stiffened, senses on high alert. His heart started thumping wildly when starlight illuminated the features of the man walking toward the rear of Izzy and Wyatt's house.

Finn climbed the steps to the porch and stopped a few feet from Alex. He jammed his hands in the pockets of his jeans, his face solemn. "Hi."

Alex swallowed, nails biting into his palms. "Hi."

Finn glanced at the swing. "Can I sit beside you?"

Alex hesitated before dipping his chin. Timber creaked when Finn dropped down next to Alex. Taut silence filled the space between them.

"I couldn't sleep, so I thought I'd come by and see if you were still awake," Finn murmured.

Alex stayed quiet.

"I love you, Alex," Finn said.

Alex's heart lurched violently. He turned and stared at Finn. His stomach flipflopped at the expression on Finn's face.

"That's what I should have said that day," Finn continued, his tone full of regret while his eyes shone with a fervent light. "That was what I was intending to say to you when I came to pick you up at your office."

Confusion flooded Alex. "What?"

Finn reached across and took Alex's left hand. He stroked the pad of his thumb across the wedding band on Alex's ring finger.

"Thank God you're still wearing it," he whispered, his voice trembling.

Alex shivered when Finn lifted his hand to his lips and dropped a reverent kiss on his knuckles.

"I know I should have trusted you," Finn whispered. "I *know* I've hurt you." He clasped Alex's hand and gazed at their linked fingers. "The truth is, what I feel for you scares the hell out of me. I've—" he paused, his throat bobbing as he swallowed convulsively, "I've never felt this way about anyone before. Not even Catherine."

A tear slipped down Alex's left cheek, his chest so tight with emotion he could barely catch his breath.

"I want to possess you, body, heart, mind, and soul," Finn breathed, his dark gaze gleaming with a burning intensity. "I want to brand you so that the whole world knows that you are mine and mine alone. I want to put you in a cage so that you can never escape my hold. And I want to hurt anyone who would ever dare try and take you away from me."

Alex shuddered when Finn gently wiped the wetness on his face with his thumb.

"That's how much I love you, Alex."

Alex drew a shaky breath when Finn moved from the swing and went down on one knee in front of him. Finn slipped a hand inside his jeans pocket and took out a pair of gleaming, silver rings. Alex stared at the beautiful, intricate design carved into the metal.

"I had these made for us," Finn explained at Alex's shocked expression. "I was going to ask you to marry me that night." A sorrowful smile curved his lips. "As in, marry me for real, this time."

Butterflies swarmed Alex's stomach.

"I know this is a lot to take in," Finn murmured. "The exhibition is tomorrow night."

Alex startled. He'd forgotten all about Finn's show in L.A.

Finn removed the ring Izzy had bought two months ago from Alex's left hand and replaced it with the one he'd had made. Alex trembled when the warm metal kissed his skin. Surprise jolted him when Finn placed the second, new ring in his palm and closed his fingers over it.

Finn gazed into Alex's eyes. "I'll be waiting for you in L.A. I'll wait however long it takes for you to put this ring on my finger and accept all that I am and all that I want us to be."

Tears fell unfettered down Alex's cheeks as Finn pressed a hot kiss to his forehead, rose to his feet, and disappeared into the night.

CHAPTER TWENTY-FOUR

He took a deep breath and forced himself to relax. He'd always hated the limelight and tonight was no different.

Carter Wilson put a friendly arm around his shoulders.

"Five more minutes and we'll be inside," the actor murmured before directing a dazzling smile at the reporters and paparazzi crowding the road outside the art gallery.

"I thought Izzy was joking about you and the red carpet," Finn mumbled. "Did she really twist your arm into coming here tonight?"

"So hard I nearly cried," Carter admitted. His eyes twinkled. "To be fair, I did want to meet the man Alex had gotten hitched to."

A sharp pang stabbed Finn's heart at Carter's words.

"Something tells me all is not well in the Garden of Finn and Alex," the actor muttered.

Finn bit back a sigh. "Did Izzy tattle?"

Carter chuckled. "Like the proverbial canary. That woman couldn't keep a secret if her life depended on it." His eyes narrowed as he spotted something over Finn's shoulder. "Speak of the devil."

Finn turned. Izzy came out of the gallery entrance, looking resplendent in an emerald dress that highlighted her eyes. She hooked her arms through Finn and Carter's elbows and flashed a dazzling smile at the press.

"Time to head inside, boys."

Relief flooded Finn as Izzy guided them away from the reporters and photographers. He accepted the glass of champagne the gallery owner handed to him as he stepped through the gallery doors and spent the next half hour greeting the guests Izzy had invited.

It was clear from the reactions of the art patrons in the room and the social media feeds Izzy occasionally showed Finn on her cell that the art exhibition was already a hit, this despite the fact that they had yet to unveil the central piece sitting under a sheet on a podium in the middle of the gallery.

Finn had just glanced at his watch for what felt like the hundredth time when Izzy sidled up to him and linked an arm through his.

"I just heard from one of the security guards," she said with a grin as she guided him toward the rear of the gallery. "Apparently, a guy on a black and red Triumph just pulled into the parking lot out back."

Finn's stomach clenched. He stared at Izzy. "Where is he?"

Izzy grinned and indicated a side passage to the left. "Take a right at the end of that corridor."

Finn's pulse raced as he practically flew down the passageway.

The truth was, walking away from Alex last night had been one of the hardest things Finn had ever had to do in his life. And every minute they'd spent apart since then had been sheer torture.

A hauntingly familiar voice reached Finn when he stepped out the back door into the balmy night.

"Look, I'm telling you I'm not paparazzi. Just tell Izzy Batista that Alex Hancock is here."

Finn's heart soared when he saw Alex staring down the security guard who stood frowning at him in the parking lot. Alex's hair was all slicked back and he was wearing a black tuxedo that hugged the toned lines of his body and highlighted his beautiful, blue eyes.

Finn's cock twitched.

Alex looked more alluring than the A-list star who had just graced the red carpet with Finn. Finn headed briskly toward the two men. They turned at the sound of his footsteps, Alex stiffening slightly.

"It's okay," Finn told the guard. "He's my husband."

He strode past the startled security man, cradled Alex's face in his hands, and took Alex's mouth in a passionate kiss, unheeding of anyone else who might be watching.

HEAT. ELECTRIFYING, ADDICTIVE, INTOXICATING HEAT.

It ignited Alex's veins in a flash and caused him to shiver as Finn wrapped his arms around him. Alex melted in Finn's hold, his body burning with desire.

All it'd taken to get him this hot was a single kiss.

That fact should have scared Alex. Except it didn't.

He'd come to L.A. to claim this man.

And claim him I will.

Alex's eyes fluttered open when Finn reluctantly ended their kiss. He hadn't even realized he'd closed them, so lost was he in the magic that was this moment. He became aware of the security guard's shocked stare and chuckled against Finn's lips.

"Hi."

Finn smiled. "Hey." His arms tightened around Alex. "You sure as hell know how to make an entrance, Hancock." He rubbed his nose against Alex's. "And, FYI, you look absolutely gorgeous."

Alex flushed when he felt Finn's growing erection against his thigh. "So do you. You sure scrub up nice."

Finn grinned and took Alex's hand. "Let's head inside."

Alex dug his heels and tugged on Finn's arm, pulling him to a stop. "Wait."

Finn looked at him, puzzled. Understanding dawned on his face when Alex removed the ring he had given him on Izzy and Wyatt's porch from his pocket. Finn's expression sobered.

Alex's fingers trembled as he removed Finn's wedding band from his left hand and slipped the one Finn had had made for them in its place.

Finn shuddered when Alex pressed a kiss to his left ring finger and the warm metal now gracing his skin.

"My answer is yes." Alex swallowed as he linked their hands together and gazed into Finn's eyes. "I accept all that you are, Finn West. And I give you all that I am in return."

Tears glimmered in Finn's eyes. He pressed his forehead against Alex's. "I love you, Alex."

Alex's breath hitched in his throat, his vision blurring his own tears. "I love you too, Finn."

A voice called out across the parking lot.

"Hey, you two!" Izzy shouted from the back door. "We're about to do the big reveal, so get in here!" She paused. "Why does the security guy look like he's about to cry?" She sucked in air. "Wait. Are you two *crying*?! Does—does that mean you're getting back together?!"

Alex chuckled. Finn grinned and dipped his chin, his fingers tightening around Alex's.

Izzy squealed. "Woohoo!" She clapped her hands and jumped up and down excitedly, her face beaming with joy. "We have *got* to celebrate this! Wait till I message the guys!"

CHAPTER TWENTY-FIVE

ALEX HEADED INSIDE THE HOTEL SUITE AHEAD OF FINN. He dropped his overnight bag on a chair and gazed at the opulent room Izzy had booked for Finn's stay in L.A.

"Whoa. This is nice."

Finn closed the door and walked up to Alex. He wrapped his arms around Alex from behind and nuzzled Alex's hair. "I asked the hotel to upgrade us while we were still at the gallery."

Alex leaned back against Finn and sighed contentedly. "Great idea."

They stayed like that for a while.

"Tired?" Finn murmured.

Alex shook his head and turned in Finn's hold. He raised a hand to Finn's face and stroked his cheek. "Thank you."

Finn turned his head to press a hot kiss to Alex's palm. "What for?"

Alex smiled tremulously. "The sculpture. It's beautiful."

Finn's eyes shone brightly. "It's us."

Alex's heart swelled at the love in Finn's gaze.

The central piece of Finn's exhibition had been revealed to wild applause and was already the talk of the town. Alex had barely been able to contain his tears when he'd finally set eyes on the dazzling alabaster artwork Finn had created from his hours of modeling in the studio.

The piece depicted a sensual male figure being caressed by another man. Even though Finn had not included anything above the neckline or below the navel, the way the two were entwined around one another and their hands touched each other spoke of their passionate feelings.

Finn had entitled it "The Embrace".

Izzy had already received dozens of offers from patrons interested in purchasing the artwork. Finn had refused all of them.

"Tell them the piece is private and will be returned to Twilight Falls," Finn had said, gazing heatedly into Alex's eyes.

It had taken all of Alex's will not to grab Finn and kiss him in front of the entire gallery at those words.

"What are you thinking?" Finn murmured presently, bumping his nose against Alex's.

Alex's lips curved in a teasing smile. "You really want to know?"

Finn grinned. "I get the feeling whatever it is is dirty."

Alex arched an eyebrow. "Why don't we head into the bathroom so I can give you a live demonstration."

Finn chuckled as Alex started hurriedly undressing him. His pupils dilated with desire when Alex stripped out of his own clothes.

"Come here," he said huskily.

He looped his arms around Alex's waist and pressed their bodies together, his erection rubbing against Alex's. Alex shuddered as Finn took his mouth in a hungry kiss. He pressed his hands to Finn's chest and backed Finn into the luxurious ensuite and the large, open shower.

Finn groaned when Alex wrenched his mouth from his to turn the faucets on. His expression grew fevered as Alex dropped down on his knees and gripped his hips, the hot water pounding their bodies.

"You look like you've had a heavy day, honey." Alex licked his lips and grinned at Finn teasingly before slowly sucking one of Finn's heavy balls into his mouth.

Finn cursed and clasped Alex's shoulders. "Fuck!"

"Oh, we'll do that in a bit," Alex said with a low chuckle. "Why don't you sit back and enjoy being serviced first, *sweetheart*." He licked a scorching path from the root of Finn's cock to his engorged tip before taking Finn's shaft inside his mouth.

Alex's cock trembled between his thighs as he tasted Finn. He palmed his aching dick and stroked himself while he blew Finn slow and deep.

Finn's fingers found Alex's hair, his hips bucking

and rolling as he succumbed to his body's primal desire and started fucking Alex's mouth.

Alex breathed through his nose and relaxed the muscles of his throat as Finn's thrusts grew hard and fast, his cock sliding deeper inside Alex. Savage grunts of pleasure ripped from Finn, his precum making Alex's mouth slick and even hotter. His hands tightened on Alex's head a moment later, the catch in his breath telling Alex he was close to climaxing.

Alex dug his fingers in Finn's thighs when Finn rose on his tiptoes and came with a violent shout, his hips pumping his dick wildly into Alex's mouth and filling his throat with cum.

Alex moaned and swallowed greedily. He couldn't get enough of Finn's musky scent and taste and decided there and then to blow him again several times over before morning came.

Finn panted and shivered as Alex let go of his twitching, spent cock and rose to his feet.

"Feeling relaxed yet?" Alex murmured against Finn's lips.

Finn swore and kissed Alex. A wild sound left him when he tasted himself on Alex's tongue. "Alex?"

"Yeah?"

"Make love to me."

Alex stilled at Finn's request. He stared into Finn's eyes, his heart drumming against his ribs.

Though he loved bottoming, Alex had topped guys before and had enjoyed the experience. He'd sometimes wondered how it would feel to take Finn but had never voiced his thoughts on the subject, uncertain if it was something Finn would even want to try.

"Are you sure?"

Finn nodded. "I want to." He bit his lip, his expression growing awkward. "Is that okay with you?"

"It's more than okay," Alex murmured, his cock throbbing at the thought of entering Finn. "And this is the perfect place to get you ready."

FINN GASPED WHEN ALEX TOOK HOLD OF HIS WAIST AND turned him around to face the tiles.

"Put your hands on the wall, Finn."

Finn shivered at Alex's commanding tone. He did as he was told, excitement sending his pulse spiking.

Alex ran his hands lightly from Finn's shoulder blades all the way down to the dip of his lower back, his fingers skimming the cleft at the top of Finn's ass with a light, sensual touch. He went down on his knees and pressed a hot kiss to Finn's left butt cheek.

Finn stiffened, his eyes widening as he glanced at Alex over his shoulder.

"Wait. Are you going to—"

He sucked in air as Alex parted his crack with his fingers. A shudder rippled through him when Alex's breath washed across the part of him that had never been touched by anyone before.

"Yes, Finn." Alex spread Finn's butt cheeks wide

open. "I'm going to do exactly that. So, why don't you face forward and enjoy the ride?"

Finn cried out at the first flick of Alex's tongue against his virgin hole, his cock hardening in an instant. "*Oh!*"

"Like that?" Alex circled Finn's twitching entrance with his tongue.

Finn dropped his forehead against the tiles and nodded jerkily, his insides tingling in anticipation at what Alex was about to do to him. Was doing to him.

"Good," Alex murmured.

Finn clutched the wall as Alex rimmed him, his tongue sending pulses of pleasure shooting through Finn's back passage. Finn let out a guttural groan when Alex stretched him open and alternated between sucking and licking his pucker, and stabbing his stiff, furrowed tongue inside.

Finn's dick throbbed and leaked precum as he started rubbing himself against the tiles, unable to curb the rolling motion of his hips.

Alex was eating and fucking his hole with his tongue like he was the most delicious feast in the world and it was driving Finn insane with pleasure.

Finn tensed when his orgasm started building in delicious waves at the base of his spine and in his heavy balls.

"Alex? I—I think I'm gonna come!"

"Then come." Alex nipped Finn's butt cheek with his teeth, causing Finn to curse. "I'll catch you when you fall."

Finn shuddered. He couldn't believe he was about to climax just from Alex's mouth on him. He hissed when Alex slipped one finger past the tight ring of muscles guarding his entrance and penetrated him.

Finn clenched around Alex, wrenching a groan from the both of them.

"Jesus, Finn," Alex growled, biting the globe of Finn's left butt cheek so hard Finn knew he'd leave a mark. "You're so hot and tight. I can't wait to get inside you!"

Finn moaned as Alex dragged his finger out before pushing it inside him again, his tongue still working Finn's rim. Finn widened his stance and hung on to the wall for dear life, his hips punching his throbbing dick against the tiles while Alex finger fucked him toward what he knew was going to be an epic orgasm.

The most intense bolt of pleasure stabbed through Finn and caused him to curse when Alex pushed his probing finger against a particular part inside Finn's passage.

"That's your sweet spot, Finn," Alex said, gnashing his teeth.

Finn trembled as Alex pressed and massaged his prostate once, twice, three times. He climaxed with a force that left him gasping for air, his cock spurting jets of cum all over the tiles while his ass spasmed and squeezed Alex's finger.

Alex waited until Finn's convulsions started to die down before slipping his finger out of Finn's body and kissing a torrid path up his back as he climbed to his feet.

Finn moaned when Alex pressed his raging erection against his sensitive hole, his body still twitching with aftershocks of pleasure.

"Let's go to the bed," Alex whispered, nipping Finn's nape with his teeth. "I want to sink my cock *so* deep inside you right now!"

Finn nodded, his cheeks and ears hot with anticipation. Alex grabbed Finn's hand and tugged him out from under the water. He dried Finn and himself briskly with a towel before leading Finn into the bedroom, his face flushed and his eyes dark with desire.

Alex pushed Finn down on the bed before walking over to his overnight bag. He took out a bottle of lube and condoms and headed back to the bed.

"Alex?" Finn said, his heart pounding so hard against his ribs he thought it would burst from his body.

Alex dented the mattress with his knees and leaned on all fours above Finn.

"Yeah?" he murmured, pressing searing kisses to Finn's throat and chest.

"I don't want the condom."

Alex froze. He straightened and stared in Finn's

eyes, surprise and what looked a lot like excitement dawning on his face. "Are you sure?"

Finn swallowed and nodded. He bent his knees and dropped his legs open, his hand sneaking down to touch the folds of skin guarding his entrance. He was already soft and loose from Alex's ardent ministrations in the shower.

"I want all of it, Alex. All of *you*."

A feral light brightened Alex's indigo eyes. "Fuck."

He leaned down and took Finn's mouth in a fierce kiss. Finn arched off the bed as Alex stroked his hands down his chest. He hummed with pleasure when Alex's nails scraped his nipples lightly.

Alex leaned down and played with Finn's stiff nubs with his clever tongue before sucking him into his hot mouth.

Finn moaned and trembled at the heady sensation. He'd never thought of himself as being a nipple man before but Alex was fast proving him wrong.

Alex worked his way slowly down Finn's body with his hands, lips, and tongue, driving Finn crazy all over again.

Finn shuddered when Alex grabbed a couple of pillows and positioned them under his lower back and butt, raising Finn's lower body enticingly off the bed. Alex kept his heated gaze locked on Finn's as he uncapped the bottle of lube and poured a generous amount in his hands. He warmed the liquid briskly between his palms, rubbed a slick layer onto his cock, and brought two fingers to Finn's ass.

Finn's breath hitched in his throat as Alex bent his right knee and pushed him open. Alex rubbed and teased Finn's entrance before pushing his fingers inside, his breathing ragged and his cock dripping with precum.

Finn panted and moaned as Alex slowly scissored his fingers and spread him open. Alex hooked Finn's leg around his left hip, reached for the lube, and poured it directly onto Finn's hole.

Finn jerked at the sinfully cool sensation, his insides clamping around Alex's digits. Alex slipped his fingers out and thrust them in again, an animal sound of lust rumbling out of him at the wet sounds their bodies made together.

Finn reached above his head and grabbed the bedsheets in a white-knuckled grip, his hips rolling off the bed as Alex fucked his hole, stretching him for the cock that would soon impale him. He gasped when Alex grabbed the back of his calves and lifted his legs in the air.

"Relax." Alex pressed a kiss on the inside of Finn's left thigh before dropping Finn's ankles on his shoulders, his pupils dilated with desire. "This angle will be easier for you."

Finn's hands found Alex's hips when Alex positioned his dick against his hole. He let out a low moan as Alex pressed home, the broad head of his cock parting Finn's slicked up folds. Finn hissed when a burning sensation filled his insides. Alex paused, his expression growing anxious where he loomed above Finn.

"Just a bit more." He closed a hand around Finn's

trembling cock and started rubbing him. "Breathe, Finn."

Finn nodded jerkily and panted, forcing his lower body to relax.

Alex gritted his teeth and pumped his hips in slow, shallow thrusts, driving his shaft deeper and deeper inside Finn.

They both groaned when he finally impaled Finn to the hilt.

Finn gazed dazedly at Alex, his pulse thrumming and sending blood pounding in his ears. He couldn't believe how fully Alex was filling him, or how right it felt to have Alex's cock inside him. Finn knew they'd be doing this again and soon.

"*Alex.*" Finn clenched his hole and drew a curse from Alex.

Alex sank his teeth in Finn's right calf and gave Finn what he wanted, his mouth opening on carnal grunts as he started fucking Finn in earnest.

Finn arched and rolled his hips, his body meeting Alex's every thrust, his heels digging into Alex's shoulders, his insides prickling with hot bolts of intense pleasure. He almost screamed when Alex's cock rubbed against his sweet spot.

The world faded around Finn as his eyes locked on Alex's hungry gaze, his orgasm so close he could taste it. Neither of them looked away from the other as Alex started punching his hips faster and harder against Finn's ass, the wet slap of hot skin meeting hot skin an illicit music that only drove their passion higher.

Sweat dripped from Alex's nose and splashed onto

Finn's chest as he rose above Finn, his lips parted on hoarse gasps and groans and his movements growing jerky.

The most incredible band of pressure formed in Finn's lower belly and caused his entire body to stiffen. Finn moaned in pleasure-pain when Alex placed the palm of one hand on that exact spot and pressed down while he drove his cock hard and deep inside Finn's passage.

They climaxed together, their shouts of ecstasy echoing around the suite. Finn's cock jerked and splashed cum all the way up his chest and neck while Alex's dick throbbed and filled his insides. Finn whimpered at the wicked feeling, his ass squeezing and gripping Alex's shuddering shaft rhythmically, drawing every last drop out of Alex's cock.

It was a while before Alex lowered Finn's legs around his waist and collapsed onto Finn, his body racked with shudders as he pushed Finn into the mattress, his heart beating wildly against Finn's chest.

"Wow," Finn mumbled, the sounds of their ragged breathing echoing in his ears.

Alex chuckled against him. He lifted his head and dropped a kiss on the tip of Finn's nose. "That good, huh?"

Finn blushed. "Yeah." He gasped when Alex punched his hips slightly where he was still wedged inside him. "Does everyone's first time feel like this?"

A chagrined expression crossed Alex's face. "Nope." He rubbed his nose against Finn, a teasing light in his eyes. "I'm just that good."

Finn laughed. His laughter dissolved into a moan when the motion caused Alex's dick to shift inside him.

"How about you fuck me next and then we can do a repeat of this?" Alex said, nipping at Finn's lower lip with his teeth.

Finn groaned when Alex slipped out of him. Heat filled his cheeks as Alex's warm cum started oozing out of his hole.

Alex's expression grew untamed when his gaze found the sticky trail making its way down the inside of Finn's left thigh. "God, Finn. That makes me want to—"

Finn grabbed Alex's waist, flipped him onto his back, and took his mouth in a heated kiss.

"I know," he whispered against Alex's lips, his heart full to bursting at the love and desire radiating from Alex's eyes.

EPILOGUE

"Are you ready?" Izzy asked Alex.

Alex bit his lip and nodded nervously. "Yes."

They pushed the chapel doors open and stepped inside the light, airy chamber. A dozen figures rose from the gaily decorated pews lining the nave and turned to smile at them. Alex looked past the faces of the people he loved the most in the world to the man who stood waiting for him at the altar.

A dazzling smile curved Finn's lips as he gazed lovingly at Alex.

Today marked the six-month anniversary of their fake marriage.

It was also the day they'd chosen to cement their relationship with a brand new ceremony.

The county clerk who'd officiated their first wedding beamed at them.

"We are gathered here today to witness and celebrate the renewal of Alex and Finn's vows. With love and commitment, they have decided to live their lives together as husband and husband."

As the clerk's words washed over their small gathering, Alex found himself remembering that day, all those months ago, when he'd first walked inside this very chapel and seen Finn for the first time.

From the misty look in Finn's eyes and the way his fingers clenched around Alex's where they stood holding hands, so was he.

"Any doubts this time, Mr. Hancock-West?" Finn murmured.

Alex glanced at the gleaming bands on their ring fingers before gazing into Finn's beautiful eyes. "None, Mr. Hancock-West." He leaned toward Finn.

"Hmm, guys?" Izzy hissed from where she stood at Alex's side. "It's too early for the kiss!"

Someone snorted in the audience. The clerk bit her lip and swallowed a giggle.

The whole chapel erupted in cheers when the ceremony concluded with Finn looping an arm around Alex's waist and bending him backward while he took his mouth in a passionate kiss.

"Get a room, you two!" Aunt Maggie shouted.

Izzy sniffed and wiped the tears of happiness brimming in her eyes.

Alex and Finn turned and shook their guests' hands as they started walking down the aisle.

Drake gazed at them with a faint smile when they stopped in front of him. "No hard feelings?"

Finn shook his head and took Drake's hand in a

firm grip. "None. You're Alex's friend. And I hope I can one day count you as one of mine, too."

The love Alex felt for Finn expanded and filled his chest to bursting as he looked at his husband.

Drake glanced from Finn to Alex. "You already are."

Emotion choked Alex's throat. He and Drake had spent long hours talking about their relationship after he and Finn had come back from L.A. four months ago. To Alex's relief, the bonds of friendship that existed between them were still as strong as ever, if tinged with regret at a love lost.

Later that night, as he lay in Finn's arms, his cock wedged inside Finn's body while their ragged breathing filled their bedroom, Alex thanked whichever twist of fate that had brought him back to Twilight Falls and to this man.

"What are you thinking?" Finn murmured.

Alex raised his head and gazed into Finn's pleasantly sated eyes. "That coming home was the best move I ever made."

Finn smiled. "And here I thought you were having filthy daydreams again."

Alex's ass twitched when he felt Finn's cock stir between their bodies. He arched an arrogant eyebrow. "I think that would be you, wouldn't it?"

Finn chuckled. "Busted."

Alex slipped out of Finn and rolled onto his back. He tucked his hands behind his head, bent his knees, and dropped his legs open. Finn's eyes darkened as his gaze locked on Alex's swelling erection and the shadowy cleft under his balls.

"Come and get me, husband," Alex breathed. "I'm all yours."

Finn grinned and pressed a hot kiss to Alex's mouth.

THE END

What happens when a sexy movie star meets the hot pastry chef next door?
Get Carter (Twilight Falls 2)

Have you read the Nights series yet? Find out if Gabe Anderson accepts Cam Sorvino's promise of one night of mindless pleasure to help him overcome his phobia of intimacy!
Get One Night (Nights 1)
Turn the page to read an extract now!

ONE NIGHT (NIGHTS #1)
SPECIAL PREVIEW

CHAPTER ONE

What the hell am I doing here?

Gabe Anderson scanned the crowded club in the mirror opposite the bar before looking down into his scotch with a self-deprecating smile. This had seemed like such a great idea an hour ago, when he'd been staring at an empty weekend in an even emptier apartment.

Saron was located in a side alley, a short walk from Shinjuku's main club strip. Despite its somewhat shady location, the place oozed style.

Gabe had hesitated when he'd seen the suited doorman guarding the entrance and wondered if access was by invitation only. He only knew of *Saron* from overhearing his clients mention it a few nights ago. From what he'd made of their excited conversation, it was *the* place to hang out in Shinjuku if you were of a particular sexual inclination.

The doorman had checked Gabe over for all of three seconds before wordlessly unclipping the rope from the stanchions framing the steel doors. He had obviously passed some kind of test, though what it was he didn't know.

Beyond a foyer with a cloakroom manned by a male attendant who looked like he'd walked straight out of a *GQ* shoot were a set of shallow steps leading to a wide, sunken floor.

Despite the butterflies churning his stomach, Gabe had stopped and stared appreciatively at the decor. As a consultant for one of Chicago's biggest design firms, he could tell how much money had gone into giving *Saron* its unique look. The club was drowned in deep reds, dark purples, and rich earth tones. Scattered across the oak floor were Brazilian cherry wood tables and armchairs boasting plush velvet upholstery and satin cushions. Discrete booths dotted the walls and afforded privacy to those who needed it, although the muted lighting provided enough of that as it was. A polished mahogany counter with wine-red leather and walnut stools ran the length of the bar on the right.

At the far end of the room, a woman in a black cocktail dress stood on a raised podium. She was crooning a song in a sultry, deep voice, her eyes closed and her glossy ruby lips glistening in the mellow spotlight. Behind her, cymbals vibrated gently, a piano tinkled, and a saxophone hummed, the sounds somehow rising above the voices of the men packing the place.

It was as he'd made his way to the bar that Gabe had realized why the doorman had let him in. From the looks of the club's patrons, *Saron* catered exclusively to an upscale clientele. He was willing to bet a week's wages none of the suits in the place cost less than five hundred dollars.

"Ah, fresh meat."

Gabe froze in the act of sitting on a barstool, his gaze swinging up to meet a pair of amused green eyes on the other side of the mahogany counter.

"Excuse me?" he said stiffly.

The bartender, a striking blond in a slate, silk tuxedo vest and crisp white shirt, flashed him a grin.

"I've not seen you around these parts before. What will it be?"

Gabe swallowed, wondering whether the man had seen straight through him and grasped the reason he had come to *Saron.*

"What will what be?" he mumbled, unable to mask the apprehension in his voice.

The bartender pursed his lips and observed him with a shrewd expression before leaning across the counter.

"Relax," he murmured in Gabe's left ear. "I can tell it's your first time in a place like this. If you keep up that deer-in-the-headlights look you've got painted across that pretty face of yours, you're gonna be a target for every sleaze ball in this club. And, trust me, they might be wearing thousand-dollar ensembles, but some of these assholes are nothing but dirty pigs in suits."

An involuntary bark of laughter left Gabe's lips at the mental image the bartender's words had conjured. The sound carried along the counter, drawing stares.

The knot of tension that had been sitting between Gabe's shoulder blades ever since he ventured into Shinjuku eased as he smiled at the bartender.

"I've never been called pretty before."

The guy winked.

"Trust me, you're the hottest thing on legs in this place right now. Besides me, of course."

Gabe chuckled and ordered a scotch, his confidence boosted by the compliment.

Two months had passed since he'd relocated to Tokyo from Chicago. When his bosses had sprung the offer on Gabe in early spring, the chance of a fresh start in a place void of the dark memories that had plagued him for eight years was too much of an attractive proposition for him to reject. He'd left Chicago with two suitcases and five crates full of books and artwork, the only things he had to show after a decade in the city.

Though he had been prepared for the culture shock, life in Tokyo had still come as a surprise, albeit an invigorating one. He had always had an interest in the country and its intoxicating mix of traditional and contemporary customs ever since he made his first business trip to the Japanese branch of the firm four years ago.

Luckily, his new position suited him to a T. He had thrown himself into his first assignment with his usual drive and passion, leading the team under him to make good on a project, one which his predecessor had only made a half-assed attempt to complete. He had delivered on time, on budget, and on schedule, despite the nearly impossible deadline. The crazy hours and weekends he had put in had not gone unnoticed, and the praise lavished on his team at the grand opening of their client's luxury hotel earlier that week was all the acknowledgment Gabe needed to realize he had made the right choice in moving to this city. The fact that the money he was making could easily afford him a two-bedroom condo in the exclusive neighborhood of Meguro didn't hurt, either.

Yet, despite having relocated thousands of miles to the other side of the world, his mind would not let go of the bite of his past. Which was why, when faced with the prospect of his first free weekend and the boxes he had yet to unpack, he had looked up *Saron*'s location on the spur of the moment and decided to take a gamble.

He had promised himself this move would not be just a fresh start for his mind, but for his body, too. That he would start taking risks in his personal life again. That he would not let the bastard who had made it impossible for him to ever have a satisfying physical relationship win.

Fifteen minutes into his first drink and Gabe wondered whether he had made a bad choice. So far, Ethan, the bartender, had helped him field a burly, yakuza-looking type with tattoos up the side of his neck, three old men with sweaty palms and bald patches, and a couple of young guys who looked barely past the legal age of drinking.

With his lean build, dark hair, and blue eyes, Gabe knew he was an attractive prospect. Add in that he was a foreigner and he was coming to the conclusion that he had become a beeline for all the men in the bar who wanted to make a conquest out of the white guy – a white notch in the proverbial bedpost. They all wanted to fuck him or be fucked by him.

A cynical half-smile twisted his lips at that thought. If only they knew.

He raised a hand to the back of his neck and rubbed the warm spot that had been bothering him for a while. Something made him look up from his drink then – call it instinct or that subconscious voice that warns of imminent danger. Movement in the mirror opposite the bar caught his gaze. Or, more precisely, a lack of it.

Stormy gray eyes pierced him from the other end of the club. They locked on him, a beam of light in the gloom. Transfixing him. Immobilizing him.

Gabe's breath caught in his throat, every muscle in his body tightening in fight-or-flight mode.

The man sat apart from the crowd, alone at a table that could have accommodated three, a tumbler full of dark liquid clasped casually in his left hand. His red silk tie was crooked, as if he had slipped a finger through the knot to loosen it. The top two buttons on his white shirt were open, revealing tan skin covering toned muscles and a hint of curls.

Gabe couldn't tell whether his hair was dark brown or dirty blond. It was hard to say in the dim light. What wasn't hard to see were the subtle and not-so-subtle stares the other men in the bar were giving the stranger.

With his stubbled face, smoldering looks, and what appeared to be an incredibly ripped body beneath a custom-tailored charcoal suit, the man looked like a king sitting on a throne, commanding a roomful of servants. Servants who appeared more than willing to either get fucked by him or fuck him if he so much as lifted his little finger.

And a man like that would not have to ask twice.

Envy and irritation flashed through Gabe at that thought, shattering the spell he found himself under. He broke eye contact, shocked by the feelings suddenly flooding him, and glared at his half-empty glass. It seemed to mock him, as if it were a reflection of his own life. A half-empty, broken shell. Incapable of touching someone or to be touched.

Gabe lifted the glass and downed the rest of the drink with an angry flick of his wrist. Fire singed his throat. He welcomed the burning sensation, hoping it would calm the pounding in his chest and the tightness in his belly and groin that told him his body had reacted to the stranger.

A full glass of scotch appeared next to his empty tumbler.

Gabe looked up at Ethan, puzzled.

A remorseful grimace flashed across the bartender's face. "Looks like we're no longer the two hottest bastards in this joint. Here, compliments of the King."

Gabe stared at the drink before slowly looking over his shoulder, his pulse picking up speed.

Gray Eyes raised his glass in a toast. A teasing smile played on his sculptured lips before he knocked back his drink.

You're kidding me.

Gabe tried to block out the heated tingle running across his skin at the stranger's cocky smirk and the way his powerful throat muscles worked when he swallowed. He turned to Ethan.

"That's his *actual* name?"

Ethan grunted. "Well, no. But the asshole sure acts like one."

There was movement in the mirror opposite Gabe.

Read One Night today

AFTERWORD

To all my friends who helped make this possible. You
know who you are.

To you, my readers. Thank you for reading Alex and
Finn's story. I hope you loved this first book in the
Twilight Falls series. I would be grateful if you could
leave a review on Goodreads or on the store where you
purchased this book. Reviews help readers like you
find my books and I truly appreciate your honest
opinions about my stories.

Make sure to sign up to my store newsletter for special
deals on my books and new release alerts. Or you can
sign up to my author newsletter instead to get
upcoming release notifications, sneak peeks, and
giveaways.

BOOKS BY A.M. SALINGER

NIGHTS

One Night - 1

The Escort - 2

Tokyo Heat - 3

Sweet Obsession - 4

Sweet Possession - 5

The Proposition - 6

Undisclosed - 7

Hush - 8

One Day - 9

TWILIGHT FALLS

Alex - 1

Carter - 2

Hunter - 3

Wyatt - 4

Drake - 5

Tristan - 6

Miles - 7

ABOUT THE AUTHOR

Ava Marie Salinger is the romance pen name of an Amazon bestselling author with a passion for writing addictive tales. Known for her action-packed and thrilling urban fantasy novels, she has expanded her repertoire with the introduction of the M/M urban fantasy romance series Fallen Messengers. Additionally, she has penned the scorching hot contemporary M/M romance series Nights and Twilight Falls as A.M. Salinger. When not immersed in her writing, Ava can be found curating inspiring music playlists, indulging in her love for nature, marveling at the latest gadgets, and savoring Chinese cuisine.

You can find all of Ava's books on her author store at
shop.adstarrling.com